THE AD GAME

To, [signature]

Eyes tue book.
I lived it for
35 years!

[signature]

THE AD GAME

A Novel

MILT LYNNES

To Carol, Chris, Kathy, Jeff and Jenny

who lived through the real Ad Game.

Wednesday

It had been a rocky storm-buffeted flight all the way from Chicago. As the plane banked right into the blackness and continued its descent toward Roanoke, Virginia, the businessman pressed his cheek against the window and peered into the blackness, but only the wing lights flashing against the rain clouds were visible. Frowning, he leaned back in his seat, tugged on his seatbelt and closed his eyes to insulate himself from what promised to be a rough landing. Turning his thoughts to a more pleasant prospect—the upcoming climax of his business career, he smiled. Having started his successful advertising agency from scratch 31 years ago, the next morning he would be honored for his achievements by his peers, the gentry of the advertising agency business. In 15 hours he would be anointed.

Unfortunately, in 15 seconds he would be dead.

In the cockpit, the weary pilot took his eyes off the rain-soaked windshield to glance at his watch. Because of delays caused by the 500-mile front of heavy May thunderstorms, the jetliner was two hours late Looking up, Paul Golliard, a 30-year veteran, was horrified to see the storm-shrouded, mountain top rush up to meet him without warning. Instinctively, desperately he jerked the controls, wondering for an instant how this catastrophe had possibly happened. The plane shuddered and lurched skyward, but too late. Seconds later the silver airliner carrying 114 passengers slammed into the rain drenched earth 42 miles north of Roanoke. A cart-wheeling fireball began to vaporize in the downpour, strewing wreckage and bodies over a half-mile radius.

Among the travelers, the one passenger of prominence was Willard J. Raffensberger, namesake and founder of W. J. Raffensberger Advertising, now called WJR. Known as Will to his friends, employees and the world at large, and referred to as "where-there's-a-Willard-there's-a-way" by himself, he was en route from his home base in Chicago to White Sulphur Springs, West Virginia via Roanoke to be honored and to speak at the annual meeting of the American Association of Advertising Agencies, a.k.a. the 4A's. Only yesterday, he had switched flights from an earlier plane, delaying his departure to catch flight 1031 so that he might attend an important client lunch downtown. Clients came first.

A few months shy of his 60th birthday, Will had everything going for him. He was a member in good standing of the very exclusive Chicago River Club, the equally selective Meadowbrook Country Club, the Indian Bluff Golf Club (men only), the Chicago Economics Club, and a trustee and director of various civic organizations.

An imposing figure at six foot three with still dark curly hair that defied a comb, his slightly longer than fashionable sideburns had framed a leading man's features. His entire being had demanded attention from men and turned the heads of women. Employees approached him with deference, head waiters welcomed him with spirited voices and car hikers accelerated from a casual trot to a sprint with his ticket. Not surprisingly, the willowy blond, 30-something flight attendant on 1031 had fawned all over him with a smile as wide as Tennessee. He was tempted, but because of the lateness of the flight he could not accommodate a diversion from his schedule.

Will had founded WJR with $2500 borrowed from his uncle. His first clients were a Pontiac dealer and a local grocery store. At 28, he was too young to be awed by the odds against his success, not even dreaming that his fledgling firm would become the 19th largest advertising agency in America, or that one day its founder would be addressing the heavy breathers of the ad industry at its annual clambake and be saluted as the "Agency Executive Of The Year."

Will was blessed with an innate sense of how things were sold and what made effective advertising. But he had learned the hard way that understanding the making of great ads was one thing, making money at it was quite another. In fact, during the last 12 months Will's irresponsible (often illegal) financial dealings had created cash flow problems that now threatened WJR's existence. In just the past few days he had worked out a rescue scheme, but that was now buried with him in the Virginia mud.

As with many bigger than life advertising agency founders who moved on or passed on, there was no one of like stature to take his place. In fact, Will had no succession plan at all. Nor had he bothered to designate a successor.

He had not intended to die.

WHITE SULPHUR SPRINGS WV, 10:20 P.M.

Forty-one miles south southeast of flight 1031's crash site, Eric and Sadie Hanson sipped on twin Dewars with a splash, listening to the five Smokey Mountain Boys drown out the sounds of the thunderstorm outside by twanging through another rendition of "Turn up the fire, turn down the sheets, I'm comin' home tonight." As the band's trademark, they always smokey-mountained their way through it at least once each night from the bandstand, perched smack in the middle of the Old White Club inside the historic Greenbriar Resort. As executive vice president of WJR Advertising, Eric Roland Hanson was attending the 4A's conference as a member of Will Raffensberger's supporting cast, there to dutifully cheer the chief's speech and lead the applause. He was also present to help broaden the WJR contacts throughout the agency business. Will had often remarked, "This is a tough business; you can't have too many friends." Tonight Eric and Sadie were ensconced in the light blue, buttery soft leather of one of their favorite booths in perhaps their favorite all time bar, scheduled to meet the arriving Will for a nightcap or two about 10:30 p.m.

"Will is really late," said Sadie. "I'm surprised he hasn't called from the car."

Eric had arranged a limo to deliver his leader from the airport. He eyed the rain pounding on the windows.

"The storm has probably slowed up all the flights," said Eric.

"Could be the plane hasn't even landed yet."

"Maybe so," he agreed. "For whatever reason, it looks like the Big Guy is a no show. No sense waiting any longer. Drink up, kiddo," he suggested.

He was anxious to head for the room where he could stretch out his aching knee and catch the sports and weather on what remained of the 11:00 news.

"What's your hurry?" countered Sadie sharply. "You don't have to drive anywhere. Let's have one more. We spend our lives rushing around in this goddamn business. This is one place where we ought to be able to relax."

She was right, of course, which didn't lessen Eric's annoyance at her response. He wouldn't mind another scotch, but what he really wanted was to relax and stretch his frame out into a supine position to take the pressure off his left knee. Eric did feel a twinge of apprehension at possibly not being present when a tired and inevitably irritable Will finally arrived. As the ultimate coat holder, loyal soldier and eager retriever for the boss, he had made a career of being in attendance while avoiding confrontations with his leader.

Sadie was constantly cajoling him to stand up to Will and get some of his own ideas into the mainstream of the company. He was the number two guy in the company, right? Easy for you to say, he would answer. *You* don't have to stand up to Will. Besides, his job was to be the Chief of Staff, a role that he was comfortable with.

Tall, dark with attractive even features, and almost black flashing eyes, Sadie could be very pushy, although when it came to all the Will discussions, she always characterized it as pushing for his career.

"If you're not ready to go, let's split one," replied Eric, signaling the waiter. After ordering, Eric glanced around the crowded cocktail scene surveying the busy, noisy tables populated by the gregarious captains of the advertising business. He smiled wryly.

"Look at this group," he said to Sadie. "People always say it's a young man's business, and when you're over 40, you're over the hill. You couldn't prove it tonight." At 58, still blessed with a head of rich blonde wavy hair, Eric noticed that most of the heads around the room were crowned with silver gray; and there were few unlined faces among the moguls and near-moguls.

These were men and women who had paid their dues, and now they were here at the current epicenter of the advertising business, telling each other how great their year was looking (even if it wasn't) and how bad their golf games were because they were too busy working. The next generation was now back at ground zero working their tails off to reach the top while the top managers were all here winding down, working the room and sipping premium brand cocktails.

After another half hour it was evident that for some reason Will wasn't going to make their proposed rendezvous.

"I don't know what's happened to Will, but my leg is killing me and I've missed the news," Eric exclaimed as he signed the check.

"Let's go."

Getting up from his chair stiffly, he unsteadily steered Sadie past the "How ya doing Eric?" crowd and headed toward the exit of the

Old White Club. He hoped Will wouldn't show up in two minutes wondering where in the hell Eric was.

Well, one of these days maybe I'll be the man in the limo, he thought. Then someone else can worry about where the hell I am.

WILMETTE, ILLINOIS, 10:25 P.M.

Andrew Miller stood in the dark street three feet from the curb, facing north along Sheridan Road. The lights from the Wilmette, Illinois police car silhouetted his coatless frame as he slowly brought his index fingers from shoulder width toward each other. His legs were spread wide and his knees were locked. Swallowing his panic, Andrew needed a stroke of luck and got it as his two fingers touched gingerly. Now he hoped that two of the Chicago North Shore's finest cops weren't going to ask him to do it again.

Instead, they switched tactics.

"Okay Mr. Miller, please walk a straight line for me."

Andrew quickly and confidently strode forward hoping his bravado and his celerity would translate into a perfectly straight walk. Even though there was no line per se to walk along, he attempted to maintain a three-foot distance from the curb.

Five minutes earlier, he had explained to the two officers that his weaving route as he drove through the Chicago suburb was the result of glancing down frequently to fine tune the radio to the day's stock market report.

Apparently his walking was straighter than his driving.

"Okay Mr. Miller. We're not sure you're 100 percent, but since you live only a few blocks from here, we're going to send you on home with a warning. And next time maybe you ought to ride the train."

"Thanks, officer," Andrew said weakly, and with proper respect. He knew enough not to continue or prolong the conversation.

Climbing carefully back into the front seat of the three year-old Jaguar, Andrew began to start up slowly and cautiously. He then decided to accelerate, remembering that everyone said the best way to spot a drunk driver was to find someone traveling way too deliberately, way too slow.

Wow, thought Andrew, he had just dodged the DUI bullet. The senior vice president and head of WJR/Chicago had, over the past few hours, downed three vodkas on the rocks then consumed several white wines at almost conveyer belt rate during a news magazine's thanks-for-the-business party in the city.

From time to time he worried—was he drinking too much, too often? Did he have a problem? His doctor at last year's physical had told him that his liver enzymes were seriously elevated from drinking, and he should cut down. His wife, Sally, was on him, too. Well, he would get to that one of these days when the pressure of the job eased up. Step one was to get home without further incident.

Glancing in the rear view mirror to make sure the squad cars were not following, Andrew began to feel almost smug about having talked (and walked) his way out of a potentially damaging situation.

Shit, it could have been awful if he had been picked up, charged and maybe lost his license. Sooner or later the word would have gotten to Will. Not good for his career.

A pair of headlights heading south jolted Andrew back to reality. In his inebriated state, his mood changed from relief to that of indignation. Those Wilmette pricks, he thought. Would they have stopped him if he were driving a green Taurus instead of a green Jaguar?

Andrew concentrated on driving an absolutely straight line, discovering that the harder you tried to drive straight, the harder it was to make it happen. Every finger movement on the steering wheel seemed to be magnified.

He wheeled left at the first side street, deciding to work his way north, block by block, through the neighborhoods. The zigzag strategy, based on the theory that the cops were never waiting for you on side streets. Besides, he thought, if he spotted a squad car, he could always pull into a nearby driveway and act like he had arrived at home. Andrew continued to zig north, hoping to avoid the gauntlet. He did. Four minutes later, he pulled into his driveway, scraping the towering and ancient oak tree on the right side for the umpteenth time. Finally he guided his car into the two-car garage safely.

The 43 year-old leader of WJR/Chicago headed upstairs to bed with a huge sigh of relief, having navigated safely through DUI territory and what could have been a career-threatening incident. He was still Andrew Miller, Chicago WJR fair-haired boy and one of Will Raffensberger's favorite golfing companions.

For a while, the combination of the vodka, the wine, the party and the encounter with the law had caused him to forget about his largest advertising account. The account relationship that was in serious, maybe terminal, trouble.

NEW YORK, 11:30 P.M.

Norman I. Steinberg slouched in the cushy oxblood leather desk chair and rested his black English, hand-made tassel-toe leather loafers on the mirror finish of the mahogany desk that seemed as large as a small aircraft carrier deck to those underlings who were called on Norman's carpet. The carpet was cobalt blue, sink-in thick, and it seemed difficult to achieve a solid stance if Norman was pissed at you. He ran his hand over his scratchy five o'clock shadow–which by now was an 11 o'clock shadow. Heaving a sigh of relief, he tugged on his tie to snug it back to the neatly knotted two-block position it had occupied when he had left his co-op on the Upper East Side 14 1/2 hours earlier. It had been another in a series of drag-ass long days of preparing for the next day's presentation to a potential new account.

At 45, Norman was senior vice president and general manager of WJR/New York, and one of the premier rainmakers in the advertising business. Tomorrow, WJR/New York would be involved in one of its biggest new account pitches in years, and Norman would be leading the charge. The office needed this win. It had been awhile since they had reeled in a big one. Winning was a narcotic for the troops and reaffirmed faith in the leadership; losing spawned panic and desertion in the trenches.

Normally, an incurable optimist (you couldn't win unless you believed you could win) Norman was apprehensive about the next day. One of the reasons had to do with Will Raffensberger. He had called Will last week to urge the chairman to appear in New York for the presentation, and he had even scripted Will's opening remarks, "I've flown in from Chicago for only one reason...just to tell you how important your business would be to our company and to me personally." Showing serious "want" in new business solicitations was one of Norman's important principles behind winning. Will had begged off, explaining that he couldn't make it because of his speaking engagement at the 4A's. In spite of the absolute reasonableness of Will's answer, Norman was angered anyway, believing that it was just another opportunity for the Midwesterner to broadcast his "I hate New York" sentiments. As a result, Norman would have to stack up his senior vice president/GM title against the CEO and president badges from the competitive agencies also soliciting the account. Not easy.

Snapping his briefcase shut, he threw his raincoat over his shoulder and headed for the door. Flipping off the light switch, the generally acknowledged top new business ace at WJR headed for the elevators and 3rd Avenue, 18 stories below, wondering about his chances of hailing a cab in the downpour outside.

All he wanted was to get back to his co-op, get his clothes organized for tomorrow and get as much sleep as possible.

Passing through the revolving door of the building, Norman spotted a cab cruising slowly only 30 feet away and waved vigorously.

"Hey! Hey!"

Lucky. Climbing inside the dingy, dirty vehicle he wiped his brow wearily and mumbled his address to the equally weary driver, a scruffy blond pony-tailed youngster who looked barely old enough to drive. Slumping back in the seat, he went over the basics of tomorrow's pitch in his mind again. What were the prospective clients expecting? They told us what they wanted from their next agency. But what did they really want? Norman knew, after years of pitching new business, that there was always an agenda—what the prospect company said they wanted in their new agency. But there was also a hidden agenda. That was the real reason they were firing the old agency and searching for a new one. There was often a substantial gap between the two agendas, and if you couldn't figure out the real agenda, you were probably dead meat. He still didn't have a handle on the hidden agenda.

Satisfied that he had done everything else to showcase WJR and appeal to the prospect's needs, Norman turned off his mind as the cab pulled up to his building.

Winning this account would be another notch in the belt in his fairly obvious and long running quest for the top job at WJR. And if he kept winning there would be no way that big shitkicker could keep him out of the corner office.

He didn't even want to think about losing.

BEVERLY HILLS, 9:35 P.M.

Marcy felt the strong, but surprisingly nimble and sensitive fingers move away from her knee slowly and begin to track northward, along the inside of her thigh. Leaning back sensuously in the leather booth, she felt a rush of adrenaline course through her body as her eyes languidly swept a 180 degree view of the Polo Lounge in Beverly Hills.

The owner of the stroking hand continued his stealthy journey toward the promised land, well hidden by the table cloth. The stroker, however, was slightly ahead of schedule.

"I'm not displeased by the direction you're taking, but why don't you wait until later to reach closure," purred the strokee.

"Just making sure we're both on the same page," grinned Bob Treadman, proprietor of a company that produced television commercials and the self-anointed Hound Dog of Hancock Park in Los Angeles.

Marcy smiled back brightly, satisfied in the knowledge that what she hoped for this evening apparently was in the cards. As senior vice president and general manager of WJR/West, she was coming off a couple of killer weeks of flailing around unsuccessfully in trying to come up with an acceptable advertising campaign for her client, Caesar's Chips. She needed a break in the action and willingly accepted Treadman's offer of an early, light dinner, followed by a nightcap at the Polo, anticipating that the evening would lead to a tension-releasing, screaming roll in the hay at her spacious condominium in Santa Monica. Her smile broadened. This time the Hound Dog pursuer was really the pursued.

Stirred by an erection that wouldn't quit, Treadman raised his hand to signal for the check. With a rather round face, trending towards beefy, he was still good looking at 52. His dishwater blond hair was combed straight back and parted in the middle, reminiscent of the look of the 30's. It was hardly the prevalent style around town, but he was very much his own man, brimming with a confidence and a swagger that bordered on arrogance. Having grown up in LA, attended USC and pledged one of the very best fraternities, he was well known around the city. This was his turf.

Bob finally got Bennie's attention for the check. He was anxious to leave, secure in the knowledge that now he was about to plant one of the prominent businesswomen on the West Coast. And a ripe and luscious specimen at that.

At 39, Marcy Ellen Gallipo was tall, almost six feet, with long straight blond hair and the proud owner of a smashing figure. She did not walk into meetings. Rather, she swept in, blue eyes flashing, long white mane tossing, definitely not your demure Rebecca-of-Sunnybrook-farm female. The body language was clear. "Cover your balls guys, you have met your match." To her feminine counterparts, the message was equally as hard, "Hey girlfriends, don't get comfortable. I'm not one of the girls. You are on your own."

Around WJR/LA, and probably throughout most of the company, Marcy was known as Sheena, Queen of the Jungle. In a sometimes, whatever-you-want business, she attacked problems and situations head on. It was important to make decisions quickly—right or wrong (who remembers later?). She often made creative judgments on the spot and announced them quickly, talking in staccato and vivid headlines.

"That story board is dog meat. Start over."

"Those colors are impossible. Junk the teal; try navy."

"Jesus, get rid of the dopey headline, who'll believe it?"

Outwardly she displayed the large ego expected of a top-flight advertising agency creative director, which she had been prior to assuming her current general manager title. Will had admired her creative acumen, loved her brashness, and had moved her up the ladder rapidly at WJR/LA, sometimes at a pace faster than she was comfortable with. While in public she portrayed herself as the total package, privately she had to keep pumping herself up. And tomorrow's conversation with the president of Caesar's Foods was going to take some serious pumping. It was all about the problem-plagued new campaign.

But tomorrow would come soon enough. Tonight was the time for her softer side, as she rose from the table and gently took Bob Treadman's hand.

"My place?" His cocky grin again.

"No, my place," she said. "I like to hear the waves pounding."

Treadman's erection began to return.

Thursday

The ringing phone jarred Eric out of his deep Dewars-aided sleep. The phone was on Sadie's side and she answered groggily.

"Hello. Who? Oh, it's for you. It's Shaughnessy."

Why would the president of the 4A's be calling me, he wondered? Eric sat up wincing as he swung his knee around to stand up. He walked around the bed, took the phone from Sadie and sat down on the bedside.

"Hi Jock, this is Eric.

"Do you, uh, know about Will?"

"What about Will?"

"I have some terrible news for you, Eric. Will's flight into Roanoke crashed last night. No survivors. It's the worst. I'm sorry."

Eric's throat tightened. For a moment he couldn't speak.

"Jock...is there *any* chance he missed the flight?"

Sadie sat up and mouthed, "What happened?" Eric waved her off angrily.

"No, Eric. I ran it down. He was checked in. He was on the flight. He's gone."

"Jesus, that's unbelievable. Who else knows?"

"Well, it's on the news now, probably all over the country."

Eric suddenly felt numb, almost as if his head and his thought process had left his body. Sadie stared at him quizzically. For a moment he was simply unable to speak. It was hard to believe that Will was gone. He never imagined that anything could ever happen to Will.

"Jock, what shall we do about Will's speech? You don't want me to give it, do you?" The moment he got it out he knew it was a bad idea.

"No. No. Don't worry about it. I'll make an announcement at the meeting this morning. I guess I'll say what I was going to say, honor Will, probably ask for a couple minutes of silence and then just move the agenda up."

"Yeah, okay, Jock." Relief. No argument from Eric.

He handed the phone back to the puzzled Sadie, who replaced it on the cradle.

"The call was about Will. He was killed in a plane crash last night. That's why he never showed for drinks."

"Oh my God," exclaimed Sadie, propping herself up on one elbow. "That's awful."

"Terrible," he added.

"He was sure?"

"Dead sure; Will checked in on the flight and the plane is down. No survivors. Jock said it's all over the news by now."

Sadie sat up. "Poor Emily. I wonder if I should call her. Where are the girls?"

"I don't know, they live in different parts of the country. I can't really focus right now."

"What's going to happen to the company?"

"I don't know. I obviously haven't had time to think about it," he said with annoyance. "I can't believe this has happened. I'm going to get my shower—maybe it will help me think straight." What *will* it mean to the company, he wondered.

Eric always thought there was a slim chance that one day he would simply inherit the job of CEO WJR. Will had talked to Eric about stepping down at 60. Barely his junior in age, Eric did not really expect (hope) that this would happen. Guys like Will simply didn't hang it up. But if the chief ever did retire, Eric always assumed he would simply take over. In his mind, no special preparation was needed, no development of additional skills was necessary. Just stay close to Will, serve him faithfully and maybe, just maybe, Eric's day would come. Now what, he thought? Will was not around to select him as his successor.

After a few minutes in the shower, Eric's head began to clear. On one hand he was devastated. He had just lost his mentor and closest business associate; and on several occasions it seemed as if they had also become friends. On the other hand, a strange feeling had invaded him. It was triggered by Sadie's question about the future of the company. The feeling was that of...elation. He felt guilty, but he couldn't erase this unwelcome burst of excitement that stemmed from the growing realization that he was the senior executive (alive!) at WJR.

As he left the shower, Eric forced a mournful look for Sadie, trying to disguise the rush he felt. Would this be the day I always hoped for, but didn't think would ever come? Now that he was the senior executive at WJR, would the mantle of leadership fall upon him?

"I've got to get organized," he said to Sadie. "Why don't you turn on the news and see if it's on."

What's the first move, he wondered? Call all the WJR offices? Half of them aren't open. I should get to the office. But which one?

"After I get dressed, I'm going down to the dining room for breakfast and get my thoughts organized" said Eric, as he moved around the room gathering his clothes and displaying an unusual amount of vigor. Strangely, his knee did not ache.

"Don't you think you ought to call the other offices first?" asked Sadie.

"I'm not sure what my strategy is," replied Eric. "I have to figure out what I want to say."

"It doesn't matter," answered Sadie. "Just get the word out and tell the managers you'll get back to them. Even if they're not in yet, you can leave voice mail."

"I guess you're right. What a mess," said Eric, calming himself.

This was complicated. He really should get through to the other offices. It's what Will would have done. Will had always taken care of the big problems. He had always taken care of Eric, too.

Now the executive vice president was on his own.

NEW YORK, 7:30 A.M.

The storm that had engulfed the East finally had subsided. Only a gray, chilly drizzle remained. Norman had awakened at 6:30 a.m. and dressed swiftly but methodically in clothes he had carefully laid out the night before, as was his custom. After a quick cup of coffee and a bagel, he was ready to head out. Taking the elevator down to the street, he was faced with hailing a cab in the rain (for some reason, the doorman was not yet on duty). Norman worried about wrinkling his suit or spotting his shoes. Today he needed to look his best and be at his best. Accounts the size of Associated Foods didn't come along every day, even every year. Again Norman cursed Will's absence. It made this pitch just that much tougher for him. He didn't ask for the chairman's help often, but this was a huge opportunity for WJR. Is it possible Will wanted him to fail? Maybe Will was even nervous about him, feeling that Norman had too much influence in the company and was becoming more important than Will himself.

Walking out of the front entrance of his co-op, Norman signaled a cab. The driver, spotting Norman, pulled over and skidded to a halt, three feet from the curb. Norman frantically danced away from the wheels to avoid getting splashed.

He climbed into the cab and brushed a few drops of water from the shoulders of his $1,800 Armani suit, then took out his spare handkerchief and wiped his shoes dry.

Norman leaned forward to give the proper directions and then pushed himself back on the tattered vinyl seat and fastened his seat belt. Buckling up was a habit he acquired after a colleague was involved in a jarring cab accident.

Norman thought about the new business presentation. What had he forgotten? Were the right people in the pitch? Do we have backup visual equipment in case the computer craps out in the middle of the presentation?

Yeah, he had thought of everything. At least everything he knew about. It was the stuff you didn't know about that killed you.

His great strength was his thoroughness. While Norman was also an extremely clever strategist, his competitors were also all smart, clever strategists and engaging presenters as well. Usually they didn't screw up.

Most of the new business competitions were close, and often it was one or two little things that determined whether you won or lost. That's why Norman's pursuit of perfection was the key factor behind his success. In training young WJR staffers, he frequently told them that in new business, "Being relentless is more important than being brilliant."

Being a top-drawer rainmaker involved a lot more than orchestrating and leading the presentations. Finding the prospective accounts was a big part of the job.

Norman was a hunter. At every party or function he worked the room to see if there was a new contact to be made, new intelligence to be gathered. He eavesdropped on conversations, listened carefully in elevators, peered over shoulders on airplanes and commuter trains and learned to read upside down across a desk.

With his almost black hair and dark, flashing eyes, an aquiline nose, and even white teeth, he was darkly handsome. And he knew it. His build was a trim, although not muscular 168 pounds, distributed nicely among his 5'11" frame. He looked the part.

Nearing his office, he glanced at his watch. His timing was okay. The pitch was at 10:00 a.m., rehearsal at 8:30. Actually, he didn't want people there before 7:30. Norman believed in letting the new business team get a good night's sleep instead of keeping them up half the night or dragging their asses into the office at dawn to rehearse. In contrast to many of his competitors, he insisted on only one good rehearsal the day before. It was important that the presenters didn't leave their game on the practice floor.

As the cab lurched sharply when it rounded a corner, Norman grabbed the strap, getting dirt on his cuff of his blue suit. Brushing it off reminded him of the presentation in North Carolina when his team traveled separately in small groups and arrived late at night. Five people showed up the next morning all in dark blue suits. Despite the jokes offered by both the prospects and the agency, the pitch team looked foolish in their "uniforms." The presentation was flat, the people were listless and WJR lost the competition badly. From that moment on, Norman always specified who should wear what in a presentation.

Norman himself always chose his wardrobe based on what the prospect, the audience, expected him to look like. If he was pitching a toy company he tried to look young, colorful and creative. A blue blazer and striped shirt would be perfect. If, on the other hand, he was presenting to a packaged goods company, staffed by Ivy leaguers, a dark blue or charcoal gray suit was the ticket. (Never brown or green). Today was a blue suit, white shirt, conservative tie day.

Norman also worried about the mind-set of the people in the prospect company who listened to the pitches. They were probably apprehensive about the process.

He and Dorine Gately, the next most senior WJR person in the pitch, had talked about it last week as they decided what to present.

"Look Dorene, let's try to figure out and answer all their concerns—at least what they seem to be looking for in a new agency. They've had their current agency for five years so they're probably nervous about changing and about choosing the right one."

"Right," Dorene had said. "So we have to make it easy for them. We have to help them choose the safe buy."

In Norman's mind, someone, whoever selected the finalists, already had stuck his neck out with the choices. It was Norman's job to figure out who that was, and then develop ways to convince him or her that WJR was the safe buy.

The cab pulled up to Norman's office building. Getting off the elevator at the 18th floor, Norman headed for his office to check his email and voice mail before turning his attention to the pitch.

After setting his briefcase on his desk, Norman turned on his voice mail. There was just one message, left only five minutes ago. It was Eric's somber monotone with the news about Will.

Norman felt as if he had been punched in the chest. He replayed it to make sure he had heard it right. Suddenly he felt guilty about cursing out Will for not coming to his aid in the pitch today. Well how was he to know? Jesus, it was hard to believe he was gone...just like that.

Ten minutes later Norman realized that he had been staring mindlessly at the wall while the shock wore off. What now? He couldn't just sit here in a trance. There was a group of people poised for the pitch. There were WJR prospects coming to the agency. He had to think about his office, about what was good for WJR.

Should he cancel the pitch? The prospect was on his way and this was a big account. Could we have some kind of an initial meeting, maybe a partial presentation, thought Norman. It's terrible what's happened, but life would go on next month and next week. Why not now? Maybe Will would have wanted the show to go on, he rationalized.

How about a moment of silence—like they did for a fallen hero at a Giants game at the Meadowlands. Silence, reverently bowed heads, then they would give the pitch.

Sure, Will would have wanted it that way.

WINNETKA, ILLINOIS, 7:47 A.M.

Head throbbing from a classic hangover, Andrew ambled painfully down the platform of the circa 1916 train station platform. Having been dropped off from the line of housewives, some still wearing housecoats, who pulled up to the curb in SAAB convertibles or Land Rovers, every morning the commuters of Winnetka streamed onto the platform like industrious ants on a food mission.

Today, while casual dress had recently swept through American business with the same velocity as downsizing, it had still not taken over the neighborhood that housed Andrew and his traveling companions. In fact, the commuters of Winnetka still represented one of the last bastions of the rep tie and the Oxford button down shirt. There was even still an occasional sighting of the once popular Ivy League suit trousers showing wide cuffs worn at least two inches above the oxblood brogans. You didn't see many leather jacketed traders. They had taken earlier trains.

Sandy-haired and sporting trendy, rimless glasses, Andrew was blue-eyed and freckle-faced, and a lanky six-three, 185 pounds. He appeared to be the clean cut Dartmouth man every matchmaking mother wanted for her daughter.

Today Andrew was training it because his Jaguar XJ convertible was heading to the shop for maintenance under Sally's supervision. Again. Andrew smiled ruefully to himself remembering that, unfortunately, he was on a first name basis with his British mechanic, Mortimer.

The southbound 8:05 screeched to a halt as the cluster of commuters surged forward on cue. Andrew unconsciously hung back near the fence as the train pulled in. He had an irrational fear of an event such as a heart attack, a stroke, or simply fainting sometime that would pitch him forward under the wheels of the oncoming train. An ignominious and untimely end.

Andrew avoided conversation on the platform, if at all possible, and he took a single seat on the railroad car's upper deck for the same reason. He would spend his entire day talking with people. The train was the one place, other than an airplane, where his associates, his clients, even his wife and children, couldn't get at him, talk at him. It was a metal cocoon of privacy.

Forty-five minutes later, Andrew arrived at his office threw his trench coat over a side chair, plopped down in his desk chair and immediately opened his computer and went to the web. The headline jumped out at him.

"CHICAGO AD CHIEF DIES IN PLANE CRASH."

A wave of nausea swept over him. He re-read the headline, then double-clicked to get the rest of the story. It was Will!

At that moment, Andrew knew his professional life, and perhaps his personal existence as well would never be the same again.

SANTA MONICA, 6:00 A.M.

Her favorite contemporary music station gently awakened her. Sitting up, Marcy flicked off the snooze alarm, which she never used—too disciplined to not make it out of bed the first time—threw back the bright yellow Charisma sheets and stepped on the plush lemon yellow carpet. She liked yellow. It helped cancel out some of the gray morning skies at her seaside condo.

She was clad only in panties, a habit since college, whether she was sleeping solo, as this morning, or in the midst of a relationship. She preferred to think of her long or short-term alliances as relationships, rather than affairs. A relationship seemed to her to be regulated existence, while an affair might lack parameters and get out of control. So much of what happened in the ad world was beyond her control, she sought a certain structure in her personal life.

Last night's event with Treadman was simply a liaison, very casual, not even close to the relationship category.

On the way to her bathroom, Marcy passed in front of the three quarter length mirror. She stopped and turned to admire herself frontally. Satisfied she hadn't aged since yesterday, Sheena, queen of the advertising jungle, headed for the shower, ready to wash off yesterday in preparation to take on again today the L.A. advertising business.

In this case she was also intent on washing off the remains of Bob Treadman, who had deposited a considerable load of jism on the front of her thighs seven hours earlier. Having brought her to a total and shattering, shrieking orgasm by alternately applying his talented tongue and fingers, Bob had then climbed on top her and came between her thighs. (She would not let him inside. Mr.-had-it-all-together had forgotten a condom.) She smiled to herself as she remembered how she had orchestrated the entire evening with much the same controlled aggressiveness as her day-in, day-out business encounters.

She started up the shower and stepped in. As always, she soaped her breasts first. They were great breasts, still firm 38D's and conical shaped with the kind of nipples that push through just enough in a jersey dress to make you notice, taking your mind off whatever you were doing. Marcy (Sheena) knew when men were distracted by her breasts.

She had ascended to her present position by outworking, out-thinking, out-maneuvering, out-toughing her male counterparts. She blasted through the glass ceiling.

Marcy's advertising campaigns were as direct and aggressive as she was. As she finished soaping herself, she thought about her first big campaign. She had skyrocketed to fame in the West coast advertising community with her advertising 10 years ago for Lava Lava body lotion. The first ad read:

"THE NEXT BEST THING YOU CAN DO WITH YOUR CLOTHES OFF. LAVA LAVA."

The follow-up ads were also highly noticed and much talked about.

"LET'S GET NAKED AND DO IT. LAVA LAVA."

"GET A LITTLE ON YOU. LAVA LAVA."

The acclaimed campaign resulted in dramatic sales increases for the product. It was the first of several award-winning efforts.

She was not only talented at creating campaigns, Marcy was adept at selling them to clients, too. It was her training as an actress that helped her perform in selling situations.

Marcy had grown up in Riverside, California, the only child of an auto sales manager and a mother who experienced uneven success appearing in television commercials. Influenced by her mother as a child, she aspired to get into acting—but serious acting—not TV or the Hollywood scene. She appeared in school productions over the years with modest success, but somehow never seemed to get the leading roles. Finally, this lack of progress led her to think about pursuing other interests, one of which was designing clothes. During high school she often spent hours creating clothing designs for "Marcy G." That would be the name of her chic, upscale chain of designer stores she visualized in Beverly Hills, New York, perhaps even Paris and Milan. Having received positive feedback on her designs from her friends, she decided to study to become a famous designer.

A textile major in college in the Los Angeles area, her first job was as an assistant buyer in a department store. After a year on the job, the copywriter who wrote the advertising for her apparel lines suddenly quit. Marcy stepped into the breach and began writing the ads herself.

To her surprise, and the store manager's as well, she was quite good at it. She also discovered that she liked being able to influence what happened with sales on her lines. It wasn't long before Marcy was pressed into service writing copy for sale ads for the entire store. A few months later she put the design idea on the back burner, moved out of buying altogether and convinced management to allow her to pen the stores' new image campaign. It was a commercial success.

Over a period of time she discovered she liked advertising better than merchandising apparel. Collecting a portfolio of her creative writing samples over a three-year period, she was able to find a position as a senior copywriter in the creative department of a mid-sized LA agency. Leaving her career in retailing, she also left behind a broken engagement to a fellow assistant buyer at the store.

Marcy had come along at the right time to make a splash in the advertising world. Women had cracked advertising barriers early on, long before they were accepted, welcome or successful in other industries.

The reason was simple. Advertising is a business that worships and desperately needs talent. The first agencies that decided to hire women almost automatically doubled their talent pool overnight.

The music ended on the clock radio and news on the hour came on.

"... And the Dow Jones closed at 10,916. Again, the headline story. An American National plane carrying 114 people crashed into a rain-shrouded mountain top in western Virginia last night just after 11:00 p.m. eastern time. At this point few details are known. Unconfirmed reports are that there are no survivors. Among those listed on the flight was Willard J. Raffensberger, advertising leader and principal owner of the company bearing his name here in Los Angeles."

Suddenly, Marcy felt weak in the knees and her throat went dry. She sank back down onto the chair at her dressing table and for several moments stared at herself in the mirror, but without recognition.

"Wow," she said softly to herself. "Wow...wow...wow." How could this happen to someone like Will?

Marcy had screwed Will's brains out seven or eight times, but she was proud of the fact that these occasional liaisons took place only after she achieved her present status as head of the LA office. These rolls in the hay were almost boringly routine, and Will Baby (as he wanted to be called in bed) always moved on—never stayed the night after the act. In each case during the wash up phase of the encounters, she always hinted to him that there would be another fuck in Will Baby's future. It couldn't hurt her career.

What now, she thought. Who's in charge? What are we all supposed to do? Marcy hurried to get dressed so she could be on her way. As one of the four 5% minority stockholders of WJR, she had work to do and as an "owner" there was some sense of urgency to try to keep the company—at least LA—on an even keel after this tragedy.

Leaving her condo and heading for her car, Marcy thought about the tough morning ahead. Shit, a big ass meeting this morning that I'm not quite ready for, and now this awful Will thing.

Turning the key and hearing the throaty roar of the Mercedes 500SL, she thought about the first problem confronting her—trying to come up with a new campaign for Caesar's Chips. It wouldn't be easy. The agency had been falling on its face for six weeks.

WHITE SULFUR SPRINGS 9:05 A.M.

Sadie wasn't ready yet, so he headed off to breakfast alone. A troubled Eric Hanson closed the over-sized white painted door to his suite and walked slowly down the hallway toward the main dining room. As he passed through the corridor surrounded by the familiar pink and green floral wallpaper, the flowers reminded him that a funeral was at hand. While Eric experienced a certain amount of real grief at Will's passing, it was now muted by the current events. He felt a growing trepidation at facing the entire ad world in the next few hours. Besides the task of accepting condolences, he was obliged to come up with the answers to the inevitable questions referring to possible succession. After pondering the possible responses without resolution, he decided to answer succession questions by simply stating that the board would meet soon to discuss the matter.

Stopping at the elevator, he ran into Alex Borosky, head of one of the large multinational advertising agencies.

"Morning Eric," said Borosky cheerfully.

"Hi Alex," replied Eric morosely. Obviously, Alex hadn't heard the news, but Eric was not about to make an announcement. They chatted briefly about the upcoming convention program. Exiting the elevator, Eric peeled off at the entrance to the main dining room. He stopped behind the braided rope and waited impatiently for the maitre d', hoping that he could be seated before he had to face his first query about Will and the future of WJR. Suddenly, he wished he had chosen to have breakfast delivered to his room. It was too late now, the maitre d' was approaching. Anyway, being served breakfast at the Greenbriar was his favorite meal. He inevitably ordered the "Old White" on the first morning of a visit. "Old White" was the Old South version of chipped beef on toast. There was nothing like it in Chicago.

"Table for one, sir?" asked the maitre d'.

"Someone will be joining me...some other, uhh, one person more" replied Eric.

Jesus, I can't think straight, thought Eric as he was escorted to his table. He sat down and waited for coffee. His purpose in starting breakfast alone was to collect his thoughts and begin to think about a plan of action for the post-Will era.

Planning was not Eric's strong suit. He had always relied on his robust looks, an outgoing personality and a reactive mind to deal with problems or issues as they arose. Stream of consciousness management, Will had called it, half-jokingly. So far it had worked reasonably well for Eric, but this was different. This was complicated. Making the right decision was critical; and now the sudden void in WJR leadership had awakened an ambition within Eric, which had been dormant for some time. While assuming there was a chance he would ascend to the top job at WJR some day, he had never thought about *wanting* the job. Now he realized he *wanted* it. Will's death represented a once-in-a-lifetime opportunity for the loyal foot soldier. And the opportunity, ready or not, was now.

Eric Hanson had grown up in the small town of Blair, Wisconsin; a hamlet nestled in the rolling farmland of the southwestern part of the state. His immigrant grandparents from Norway had settled in the area and subsequently engaged in a variety of occupations, ranging from logging to carpentry to farming. Eric always believed Will had a soft spot for him because of his Norwegian origin. ("A fellow Scandihoovian" Will would introduce him.")

The Hanson clan finally settled permanently into farming and there never seemed to be an opportunity or a reason to move the family, which included Eric and an older sister, to a more prosperous town. Growing up in the 50's, there was little else to do in Blair, population 306, elevation 859 ft., except play sports, drag race on the country roads, and chase a limited assortment of pig-tailed, bobby soxed, perpetually giggling girls.

As Eric was growing up, at least half of the senior adult population of Blair still conversed in Norwegian on a daily basis. Although

Eric's parents were fluent in Norwegian, they always spoke English in his presence. In their minds, this was America, not Norway, and Eric must find his way in this world, not the old one.

By the time he got to the County High School, Eric was finding his way quite nicely. At 14 years of age, he was six feet, 160 lbs, broad-shouldered and big boned. Square featured, blonde and rangy, looking like a Norwegian Viking except for the flat top crew cut, he was a high school athletic director's dream.

Eric felt sorry for high school kids today, as most of them had to declare early which sport to specialize in. Then they had to attend a succession of camps to try to make traveling squads and all-star teams. They were all trailed by clusters of involved, often screaming parents.

Fortunately for Eric, everything came more or less naturally to him and, like a lot of kids in the 50's with athletic abilities, he played all sports. The big guns in school all played football and basketball in fall and winter. In the spring you played baseball or ran track. Nobody played golf. In Wisconsin in those days, there was no lacrosse team and only sissies messed around with soccer.

If you didn't play any sports, you were considered a clod, a fairy, or even worse, a brain.

It was high school sports that really helped Eric become a leader in high school. He was captain of both the football and basketball teams and was president of the senior class. He was the most popular boy in the school. When he reflected on those times in later years, Eric realized they were the best years of his life. Things had been downhill ever since. Even today, when he ostensibly had a big job in a big time company, Will had always been "the captain," not Eric.

He now realized he desperately wanted the CEO job. It was his best chance, his only chance to recapture some of the glory of his youth.

"Are you ready to order, sir?" asked the dining room waiter at the Greenbriar.

"I'll have the Old White," replied Eric. Realizing how hungry he was, he decided not to wait for Sadie.

What did he have to do to become CEO of WJR? Would just taking over and acting the part be enough?

Probably not. Not with that sonofabitch Norman sniping at him from New York.

CHICAGO, 8:32 A.M.

Having regained some of his composure after the Will news, Andrew picked up the *Chicago Tribune* and turned to the Ad Biz column by Horace Newman. Unfortunately, ENNU (and, therefore, WJR) was today's news. Will's accident would not have made the column; its deadline was the previous day in late afternoon.

"Is ENNU playing footsie with BBX?" read the headline. The column went on to say that "ENNU, the third largest athletic shoe manufacturer reportedly has been talking to several agencies about its advertising account. The Goshen, Indiana company has lost market share and seems to be pinpointing advertising as one of the primary causes. Sources say that BBX is reportedly one of the agencies that has had conversations with Simon Slater, new CEO of ENNU. BBX had been the runner up to WJR in the agency competition three years ago."

Andrew was crestfallen. What had been a secret contained within the agency was now on the street. The agency rainmakers in Chicago would be getting out the atlases to find out where in the hell Goshen, Indiana was. They would call their Information Centers and be on the Web to collect athletic shoe data, trends, market share figures and the list of key ENNU personnel. .

What a fucking business this is, Andrew reflected, in a rare moment of self-pity. What other industry reports on accounts that are shaky? If a box salesman were in danger of losing $1.2 million revenue of E-flute containers, would some columnist make it the lead item in his column? What was it about the ad game? Why did I get into this business anyway, he wondered.

As a youngster, Andrew had been basically a shy person. Later in life he forced himself to learn to be more outgoing as his job in advertising required.

Growing up in a tree-lined suburb of Chicago, Andrew's formative years were largely uneventful. Besides modest athletic accomplishments, he joined the Boy Scouts, went to summer camps and managed to garner reasonably good grades. He got into the usual number of scrapes with the authorities and he learned to drink beer on the beaches of Lake Michigan. He had the typical liaisons with the opposite sex, and like all of his pals he was engaged in the constant quest to get into his dates' pants. In that arena you needed to be willing to report your progress to have any standing in his group.

Andrew also learned to smoke, to drive a car, to drive a car while holding a beer, and start a car without the ignition key. In short, he was one of the guys, and while not one of the ringleaders, he always seemed to be around the center of things.

His mother had always wanted him to attend Dartmouth. Andrew never knew why this was so, but it was something she talked about over the years. He did apply to Dartmouth. There was a problem, however. His father's business was not doing well. The solution available to him was the Navy ROTC program. He was not enthusiastic about giving up his summers or committing after graduation to the service, but there seemed to be no choice. Andrew applied again to Dartmouth through the ROTC. He was indeed accepted at the Ivy League school, although the family had to sweat it out right down to the final deadline.

At Dartmouth one event was the beginning of something that helped shape Andrew's mind-set about himself. It began on the second night he was on campus. His newly assigned roommate, Alan, had rowed on the eight-man varsity shell at a Massachusetts prep school. That night Alan was on his way to a meeting to sign up for the Dartmouth crew team, and encouraged Andrew to tag along with him. Although Andrew, on his own, would never even explore this low profile sport, he had nothing else to do and knew no one else at Dartmouth yet, and so he followed his roommate to this organizational meeting.

He was intrigued with the team aspect of crew and stuck with Alan through several organizational meetings and workouts. To his amazement, he made the freshman crew team in the number two shell. Being relatively tall, he was ideal for crew, and he came to understand that it was a sport of leverage as much as strength. Most of all he learned it was a sport of endurance, and he began to run six miles each morning before going out on the water to practice.

In spite of the brutal workout schedule, Andrew grew to love his new sport. It was the ultimate team activity. With eight oarsmen rowing in total unison, you could be neither too slow nor too fast for the others, or it would slow the shell.

Most of his teammates had rowed in prep school and had an obvious head start in both technique and experience. So, Andrew figured out that the only way to catch and surpass his competitors was to outwork them. This he resolved to do. His perseverance paid off and he progressed over his years at Dartmouth to the number one varsity shell stroke, and ultimately captain of the crew team. For the first time in his life, he was the leader. As someone who had always drifted along, he had let the world come to him. Whatever happened...happened. It was his success in crew that caused him to develop his personal mantra for success in his career later. Be a team player, but outwork the other players.

Andrew met Sally during his junior year at a crew race. The Charles River in Boston was lined with striped tents and college boathouses. The Dartmouth shell had placed a strong third, and the eight athletes were raising their frosty mugs in the green and white striped tent. That's where Andrew first saw Sally. In the same year as

Andrew at Smith, she was the sister of one of his teammates and had come with her parents to visit after the race. Andrew was smitten immediately by the preppy, smiling, vivacious blonde, and from that moment on he pursued her with the same fervor he displayed in pursuing success at crew.

They were married shortly after graduation and after Andrew received his commission in the Navy. Following a brief honeymoon on Cape Cod, Andrew and Sally headed to Hawaii where he reported aboard a destroyer at Pearl Harbor. Both of the newlyweds found Navy life to be an exhilarating experience. As a division officer Andrew was now indeed a leader of men. At sea, particularly when he was on watch underway as Officer Of the Deck (OOD), Andrew felt a sense of pride and purpose as the man in charge of several hundred men and this gray metal weapon that sliced purposefully through the choppy sea. Fortunately, during Andrew's tour of duty, no one was shooting at him.

Sally became close to several of the other wardroom wives and was the ideal spouse at all the ship functions. Toward the end of his tour of duty, the couple considered staying in the Navy. Shipboard life appealed to Andrew's team concept ideals, but in the end, the uncertainty of where they might be sent on subsequent assignments was the key fact in deciding to opt for civilian life.

After Andrew's stint in the Navy, it was Sally's brother who found Andrew a job in a New York agency as an account service trainee. Andrew discovered quickly that he liked advertising a lot, but he was intent on coming back to the Midwest. He answered an ad in *Advertising Age* for WJR, which was looking for assistant account executives. There were two openings and he managed to win one of them.

Andrew's mantra of outworking his peers soon drew management's attention. He was in the office early and left late, and it wasn't long before was identified as a "comer." Every job he was given, he accepted cheerfully and he executed almost flawlessly. The promotions happened steadily over the years. He had become general manager two years ago, and things had progressed nicely. In fact, during the first year, the office grew more than in its previous three years, and it seemed to Andrew that he had a pretty good handle on this general manager thing. Lately, however, reality had set in. The office was still growing, but there had been a couple of setbacks recently. Now this ENNU problem was front and center.

Andrew stared again at the picture on the masthead of the newspaper column. Horace smiled at him. How did Newman do it? How did he get his information? Andrew knew that one of his tricks was to telephone senior people in agency after agency with the lead in of "I understand you're in on the ENNU pitch." A vehement and honest denial usually brought immunity. But any hesitation by the agency executive and Horace went for the throat, asking further questions until he wrangled an admission from the executive that yes, his agency was indeed involved. Once Horace got a "hit" he would then probe, "I understand Becker & Becker is also in the running." Often the executive blurted out agreement or denial about competitive agencies and Horace had another piece of the puzzle.

Andrew put down the paper and returned to his computer. Again, the headline reverberated with the news about the plane crash. What an utter mess. ENNU in trouble. Now this tragedy with Will. Putting the computer to sleep, Andrew leaned back in his chair and remembered to check the rest of his world. He activated his voice mail.

"Andrew, it's Eric," said the voice in a hushed tone. "Have you heard the news?"

WHITE SULPHUR SPRINGS, 9:35 A.M.

The spacious dining room was beginning to fill up with a stunning selection of sportswear with the wearers identified by name badges. The golfers of the 4A's were already dressed for their afternoon on the links and the tennis players would be attending the business sessions in tennis shirts and sweaters. Many of the 4A's attendees were seeing old acquaintances for the first time–the storm had played havoc and delayed a good portion of the travelers.

Eric's "Old White" breakfast and Sadie arrived simultaneously. He turned off his cell phone.

"Want some of this?" he asked Sadie, as she seated herself with her back to the window.

"You know I hate that stuff," she said. "I'll have the fruit plate with some yogurt, strawberry yogurt," she said to the waiter. "And, oh yes, please send the bun lady over right away." The pumpkin buns were her favorite.

"Well, what have you have figured out?" Sadie asked.

"There are two things I'm thinking about. One is the pure logistics of what happens next. Getting the word to all of our people, the clients, that kind of stuff. While that's a problem, it's doable. I've already called the Chicago office. The other thing is a big problem—having a board meeting to elect the new CEO."

"What's the problem? You're next in line, the only executive vice president in WJR. You reported directly to Will. You're senior to the general managers, right?"

"Technically, you're right. But I've been kind of a staff guy. As line managers, they reported directly to Will. He's been the one who's been telling them what to do."

"Yes, but you have more stock than the general managers."

"Only 12.4%. Just a few percent more than Andrew and Norman and Marcy. They all have five percent. But that's not the point," replied Eric.

"What *is* the point?"

"Look. Here's the thing. In our company, the other stockholders—Andrew, Norman and Marcy—are also directors."

"But you have twice as much stock as any of them," interrupted Sadie. "More than twice as much."

"That's true, but the amount of stock you hold doesn't make any difference. Our by-laws are set up so that each director has one vote on board matters, regardless of how much stock they own."

"So all the votes are equal? You never told me that before," said Sadie sharply.

"It wasn't *important* before. Will wasn't *dead* before," snapped Eric, becoming irritated.

"So how much stock you own–or don't own–doesn't matter. Anyone can be elected CEO?"

"That's right, if they get the votes."

"How many votes are there?" asked Sadie.

"There *were* seven," replied Eric. "Obviously, now that Will is gone there are six. What's really bizarre is that this voting thing has never been an issue before. Even Will only had one vote. So he always had his vote and mine, of course. Plus, long ago he added two outside hip pocket directors, just in case. Nothing ever came to a vote since everyone knew he always had a majority of directors anyway."

"You mean these two outside director guys also have a vote equal to yours?"

"That's right."

"That's stupid. What do *they* know? That isn't fair."

"I know it isn't fair," snarled Eric through clenched teeth. "I told you, it wasn't important before."

"How did all those younger people, these general managers, even get 5% of the company? You've been with Will from the beginning."

"Will wanted to lock his managers into the company. This business has gone crazy–there's a lot of job movement, and not a lot of loyalty. So as an incentive to stay with WJR, he bonused money out over a five-year period so they could afford to buy 1% of the stock a year. After the five years he made each one a director."

"Okay, so each one of the five per centers has a vote. How do we swing them?" asked Sadie.

"First, we have to figure out which of the three are competitors for the top job and who might be on my side."

"Well, who else would want to be CEO?" asked Sadie.

"Norman for sure. He's always been an ambitious sonofabitch. It seems to me he's been trying to push his way up the ladder for years. Maybe Andrew would want the job. He's always been kind of the company cheerleader. Probably thinks he could run the company someday, maybe even now."

"How about Marcy?"

"I don't think so. She probably doesn't see herself as the CEO. Not at this point of her career anyway. She's the newest GM and runs the smallest office. No power base. Besides hardly any good-sized agencies are really run out of LA. It's too flaky out there."

"Besides, this is mostly a guy company," noted Sadie.

"Well, yeah," he admitted somewhat sheepishly.

"But she is an important swing vote," said Sadie. "And so are the two outside directors, right?"

"Right," said Eric frowning.

"What about the outside directors? Could one of them be elected?"

Eric had not thought about that. "I think so, if the votes were there. I don't think the by-laws would block it. But I can't imagine that would happen."

"But it could happen."

"Yeah, it could. So I better not ignore that possibility."

He didn't yet know how he was going to put together all the votes. He added the thoughts to other notes he had scribbled on a piece of paper that he called "Operation UFFDA." UFFDA was a Norwegian exclamation that meant a lot of things. But first, there was a matter of finding out about the funeral arrangements for Will, calling a board meeting, and a myriad of other details.

Perhaps if he could handle all of this adeptly, it would demonstrate to the other directors that he was the obvious choice to move up.

Looking around the room, Eric sensed that the word about Will had spread. Familiar faces that under normal circumstances would smile, accompanied by a wave, now looked quickly away or down at their french toast.

The waiter brought Sadie's breakfast. They ate in quiet, both lost in thought.

Sadie finally broke the silence. "So, except for Miss LA, everyone including those outside guys is a competitor for the top job."

"Maybe I can't totally ignore her, either."

"This is going to take some doing," added Sadie.

Eric sighed audibly. What had at first seemed so simple, had now become very complex.

Anything could happen.

LOS ANGELES, 7:45 A.M.

Marcy pulled out onto the freeway feeling the welcome surge of power from the 500 SL that was needed to squeeze into a gap in traffic. The car phone rang.

"Hello."

"Good morning, Marcy."

"Raul, how are you? Where are you?" asked Marcy.

"I'm between Riverside and San Bernardino, on my way to the plant. I wanted to know when I'm going to see the TV for the new blue corn tortilla intro." Always direct. Not much on small talk.

"It's looking good, but we still have some fine tuning to do. We should be able to show you something Monday or Tuesday."

Raul Issac Coronado, Chairman of Caesar's Chips, smiled wryly and Marcy smiled wearily, both at the same time. Raul suspected what Marcy knew. The creative plans had not yet been developed. In the ad game it often took a firm and pressing deadline to provide the real thrust for the creative department to get cracking. Often, the creative juices didn't really flow until the countdown to the presentation date was inside a week.

"Raul, I'm on my way in now. As soon as I huddle with MJ, I'll give you a firm date."

"Actually, that's not the only reason I called. I want to know how you're coming on the re-do of the restaurant style chip campaign, too. If your agency can't come up with the campaign for the basic product, how can you expect to do the job on a new product like the blue chip?" The words were clipped. The voice was sharp.

Marcy heard Raul's voice harden. So far, WJR had presented three programs for Caesar's Restaurant Style Tortilla Chips. Raul had trashed them all, and with good reason, Marcy knew. The stuff simply wasn't good enough yet. It was bland. It had been done before. It didn't set the brand apart. In fact, the entire creative department, 20 teams, had been crashing, competing to come up with the restaurant chip advertising, which, of course, was why the agency had not yet begun the blue corn introductory campaign.

Raul was sure he knew where WJR was with both of his campaigns. They didn't have shit to show. He had been right to press Marcy for a solution. He believed the only way to get great work out of an ad agency was to always prod the creative people, demand that they meet deadlines, keep pushing them to the wall.

You couldn't let the agency get complacent. It was important to make them worry about losing the account to keep them on their toes, and keep a flow of new ideas coming.

The problem with his last agency was they had no guts. Towards the end of their relationship the agency simply tried to find out what he wanted and then give it to him. The work got worse and worse.

He liked the way Marcy stood up to him. But that didn't mean he was going to back off and give her and her people a chance to relax.

After all, he was the client.

"Marcy, are you sure you're big enough to handle the restaurant chips and the blue corn new product campaign at the same time?"

The thinly veiled threat was obvious. Caesar's wasn't the biggest account in the WJR shop, maybe third or fourth in size, but from a prestige standpoint, it was the agency's West Coast flagship account. Which is why every agency in LA had it perpetually at or near the top of its new business prospect list. The work an agency did on Caesar's was very visible in the LA market. That was important—the creative people who did the work loved seeing their stuff all over the local television scene.

"Raul, you know we've always come through for you before," purred Marcy.

"Yeah, that was then. This is now," countered Raul. "I wasn't losing share then. I am now. You know I've always resisted increasing our slotting allowances because our brand name has been so strong. But those east coast guys are starting to eat my lunch. No pun intended. And if I can't get the right campaign out of you, maybe I'll have to shift a hunk of advertising dollars into buying the shelf space while someone comes up with the right advertising campaign."

Marcy caught the *someone*. Some other agency.

This was not a discussion Marcy wanted to have over a car phone.

"Raul, we're going to nail this campaign and the blue corn intro, too. Why don't we have a quiet dinner soon and talk about this branding versus slotting allowance allocation. I've got some ideas for you."

Marcy had no ideas on this area. However, one of her business techniques was to use a promise to force a deadline. The deadline always energized her. Marcy loved telling people that over the years in creating client programs she was probably only a few hours ahead of the client.

"Do you have a time in mind for dinner?" asked Raul, his voice changing perceptibly from a business to a personal tone.

Marcy had tantalized Raul in many ways during their business meetings and, on occasion, during a business lunch or dinner, but had never let the relationship get personal.

"I have any time before Wednesday open. You pick the night."

"I'll get back to you," replied Raul, his tone warming.

She wondered, was Raul looking for an invitation? Christ, if she was going to fuck ordinary guys like Bob Treadman, should she go down for someone when it meant something? Caesar's was important, and Raul was a tough cookie. Would she have to sell the creative lying on her back?

CHICAGO, 9:30 A.M.

Edwin N. "Sandy" Bunker put down the telephone, leaned back in his black leather and burled walnut trimmed chair and closed his eyes. He was thoroughly dejected. The president of Chicago Mercantile Bank had just learned that he had lost both a customer and a friend. What an unbelievable shock—he had just seen Will the end of last week. Over the years he and Will had played golf together and also socialized from time to time. The banker would miss those times together with the gregarious and engaging agency chief. But while they enjoyed each other's company, the real basis of their relationship was business. As Bunker reclined in his chair, eyes still shut, a strong element of worry invaded his depression.

He presided over what was the lead bank for the WJR Advertising Agency. The source of Bunker's anxiety was the knowledge that WJR had recently been into well over $9 million on their $10 million line of credit. In fact, the agency was dangerously close to not making ends meet. Also disturbing to the banker was Horace Newman's morning column about the ENNU business being in jeopardy. Bunker knew that the account represented almost 25% of the revenue of WJR/Chicago.

Losing this account would undoubtedly put the WJR/Chicago office in trouble. Probably big trouble. Add that to the agency's rising indebtedness at Chicago Mercantile … and now losing their leader. Suddenly this had become an extremely worrisome situation.

Bunker was tied to WJR's fate in a personal way. He had supported the establishment of WJR's line of credit, and stuck his neck out for Will over the objections of several members of the Mercantile loan committee. Bunker had another personal connection. He was one of two outside directors of the now leaderless WJR Board.

And a key influence in the selection of Will Raffensberger's successor.

NEW YORK, 11:15 A.M.

In Norman's mind, the new account pitch that day did not go well. In fact it seemed to go quite badly. For some reason the two prospective clients seemed preoccupied, bored, or both. One, the heavy-set type, while reasonably attentive, asked few questions, and the ones he did ask seemed to have no bearing on the process of selecting the right advertising agency.

"How many people do you have in your account service department?" he asked at one point.

Why some people asked that question was beyond Norman. You didn't need an army to develop a real understanding of the client's business needs. A few smart people crystallized all the marketing information into a creative brief—a single statement of purpose—that the creative teams could relate to and work with.

"We have almost 90 people in account service," answered Norman confidently. "But the important statistic is that we have one senior person," he gestured at Dorine Gatley, who straightened up slightly and smiled brightly, "and two support people" he waved toward the two fresh-faced young account types sitting toward the end of the highly polished dark wood conference table, "who have direct experience in your business category."

The prospect who asked the question glanced at the account team and nodded approvingly, one of the few positive responses of the morning.

Norman was pleased with his answer. He had learned two things over the years about answering questions in a new business solicitation situation. One was the politician's spin of telling the questioner the answer the agency had wanted to give, no matter what the question was. The other thing Norman had learned was not to over-answer; not to say too much.

"Are there any more questions?" Norman asked.

"Don't think so," the younger, slender prospect had said, laconically. "We've learned everything we wanted to know. Thank you for all your efforts."

"Very nice presentation," added his heavy set associate.

Norman's heart sank. Their statements smacked of faint praise. It was time for him to wind-up his upbeat, new business self to try to elicit a positive response. "Thanks so much for including WJR in your search," said Norman flashing his best smile, while everyone shook hands all around. He steered the prospects toward the front lobby. In a rehearsed move, the other agency staffers peeled off to their offices. On the way out, Norman probed once more, "Is there anything, any area you're interested in that we failed to cover?"

"Nope," said the slender one. "You were very thorough."

"I can't tell you how important your account would be here. I just want to remind you that I personally would work on the business on a day-to-day basis," added Norman eagerly.

When they got to the lobby, the receptionist was standing, waiting for them wearing a bright blue dress and a broad smile.

"Your car is downstairs, gentlemen," she said, handing them each a blue umbrella with WJR logo.

Norman had thought of everything. The limo to LaGuardia, the umbrella that would provide cover from the drizzle during the few steps from front door to car, the remembrance from Tiffany and the "Why WJR" binder, which would be waiting on the seat in the limo.

As the prospects left through the double glass doors, Norman sank into the closest blue leather chair in the reception area, emptied, exhausted and puzzled.

The feeling that the meeting was a bomb persisted. There was almost no visible response from the audience during the upfront "This is WJR" portion of the presentation, and little more while his team talked about Associated Foods, its problems, and its opportunities. Norman's rule of thumb was "talk one-third about us and two-thirds about them." In this case, even the "them" stuff fell on seemingly deaf, disinterested ears.

"You wonder why they came at all," said Norman aloud. The receptionist looked up and smiled shyly. Norman had covered "the-show-must-go-on" and "Will-would-have-wanted-us-to-have-this-meeting" with proper sadness and deference. Had this offended them? Didn't seem to.

He remembered the steel company they pitched in Pennsylvania. That was like today. Their conference room table had appeared to be created out of small steel beams and the carpet and chairs were fashioned in various tones of gray. The dozen or so prospects also seemed to be forged out of some sort of metal. They didn't respond, didn't smile, and hardly said a word, as the WJR presenters showed them at least 20 different ways to market today's steel. There were almost no questions during the Q&A afterward. The pitch team left the gray room in a dejected state–they couldn't wait to get outside into the sunshine and away from what seemed to be a humiliating defeat.

Norman got the phone call two weeks later telling him WJR had won the business and inviting the agency team to the offices of the new client to review the WJR ideas that were presented. At the meeting the two top clients trashed every one of the ideas and informed Norman that WJR would have to start over. To this day, Norman was still not sure why or how they had won the steel business. (It was still an account, and a good one.)

He needed to be alone for a while, just as when he was a kid.

As a child, Norman was considered a brain. Good grades came easily to him with a minimum amount of study. Even so, his domineering father kept after him. Think how much better you could do if you worked at it. Answering that he was doing well without working at it was not the reply his father wanted to hear. Better grades were "the prelude to getting into med school" an idea that freaked Norman out. He spent a lot of time in his room, alone. Away from his father.

He knew that he would never quite measure up to his father's expectations. A skilled physician, the senior Steinberg was a third generation—and prominent—resident of Scarsdale, New York. Norman's older brother, Nathan, had become a lawyer, a profession much more to his father's liking than advertising. In fact, his father did not regard advertising as a profession at all, but rather as a job.

Nathan was taller than Norman, and possessed a more athletic body. He was a cross -country star in high school and later in college. His father was forever cajoling Norman to emulate Nathan's ambition and also his perseverance, the quality inherent in the long distance runner. Norman indeed was a very persistent type. However, no one, including himself, recognized this as one of his strong qualities during his formative years. A voracious reader, the young Norman would rather curl up with a book than pursue athletics. He was, however, an important member of the high school regional champion debating team as well. It wasn't that Norman saw himself as an orator, he simply loved to argue.

While Norman was distanced from his father, he was very close to his mother, who was a talented amateur photographer and a breeder of dogs. Privately she encouraged Norman to read.

Upon graduation from NYU, Norman went to work in a large publishing house in New York, hoping to work toward becoming an editor. It wasn't what he had in mind. Eighteen months later he ran into a college chum who was in the midst of a training program for one of the large New York advertising agencies. The agency had just won a huge automobile account. They needed bodies right away and quickly moved Norman's friend and others out of the training program and up into the front lines, which opened up several places in the training program. Norman interviewed and secured one of the training positions with surprising ease. His good looks and presentation skills immediately marked him as a "suit"–an account man. His career in advertising was launched.

In the next couple of years, Norman discovered that he had found his calling. The advertising business seemed to be peopled with well-educated, interesting people who were stimulating to be around. Norman and the other junior account people worked incredible hours, which was part of the corporate culture. Top management lived to work, and if you wanted to get to the top, you had to emulate the style and work habits of the people already there. Sixty and 70-hour weeks were not uncommon. In this environment Norman discovered his unwavering persistence was one of his greatest assets.

After a couple of years at the agency, Norman fell in love with Jasmine Kaplan, a young lawyer. She was attractive, smart, and driven, like Norman. They were so alike; it seemed to both of them that marriage was inevitable. Jasmine was the professional person that Norman wasn't and his father was reasonably pleased with the union. Unfortunately, the marriage lasted barely three years. They were both working killer hours and rarely saw each other, and when they did, they were usually exhausted. Instead of the romantic Saturday night dinners anticipated and relished by other young working couples; for Norman and Jasmine, it was an opportunity to compare calendars and make plans.

It wasn't that the couple fell out of love; they could not make the marriage work. There was no time for each other and there was no time to work at making more time. Marriage just got in the way of their careers. They simply parted, reluctantly, but eager to throw themselves separately and totally into their respective jobs.

He had learned two things about himself since high school. One was that he was truly ambitious, a quality that had been almost totally smothered or disguised by his resistance to the wishes of his domineering father. It was difficult to succeed when an authority figure kept communicating that you were failing. Away from his father's incessant carping, Norman began to experience some triumphs. At last, he found that success for him was possible.

Norman's other discovery was that he was made for the advertising business.

The day he was promoted to VP, he knew he wanted the top job in an agency. He liked being in control of lots of people and the destiny of big projects. Norman moved jobs three times before landing at WJR/New York. While more money was always a factor in his job moves, the real motivation was broadening his experience and his skills and preparing him for top management.

His inability to please his father (someday he would show him!) was always in the back of his mind. The mocking, "Advertising isn't a real profession" was a headline that he could not forget. His failed marriage was also there in the shadows of his mind.

While Norman had difficulty in forging strong relationships with those close to him, he also found it difficult to bond with business associates and acquaintances. He told himself he was too busy to be involved outside of work. So there were no pals to play touch football with in Central Park on Sunday morning. No one to drag him away from work to Yankee games. He rarely had a beer with the troops after work unless there was business to be discussed. His relationships with the opposite sex tended to be infrequent and short. From time to time he worried that he might be a latent homosexual (occasionally he seemed to attract them), but each time he had a woman in bed, he realized that this was not the case. Because his accomplishments were not measured or acknowledged by friends or loved ones, Norman badly needed symbols and trappings to signal his success. He was all Armani and Sulka and BMW. His co-op occupied one of the toniest addresses (he was in way over his head) and his art collection consisted of names you know. He had planned his rise in advertising carefully, and now he was ready for the next big move upward. Norman intended to become CEO of WJR, the ultimate success symbol.

As he turned into his office, he turned his thoughts away from Associated Foods and toward the mission. His voice mail was flashing and his email was blinking with a screen full of messages. First, better email the employees about the Will situation. There couldn't be anything more urgent than dealing with the death of the chairman.

He was wrong.

One floor below, Allie Lombardi, WJR/NY print advertising production manager and sender of one of Norman's messages, sat behind his desk. He was in a sullen mood after a conversation with Vandy Cromwell, a trusted lieutenant in his department for 20 years. Allie's mood had alternated between despair and almost uncontrollable anger during the two-minute conversation. Despair at the thought that the agency was in deep shit with a client; anger at the cause, Vandy.

He had just emailed Norman and was waiting for the shit to hit the fan.

To: Norman
From: Allie
Subject: First Affiliated

Norman. Weaver just hand delivered a letter from the chairman of First Affiliated Bank. The letter accuses the agency of receiving major kickbacks from a large printer in New Jersey. The letter is addressed to you—with a copy to Weaver and another copy to Will in Chicago. Weaver started with me—I guess he wanted to find out what was going on before he went to you. It looks like they found the irregularity during a routine audit at the bank, which included a spot check of WJR vendors. The discovery was that one of the vendors of the agency—a company whose services were invoiced through to the client—was non-existent. The clients' payments to this phantom company matched the amounts later deposited into the First Affiliated Bank account of one, Vanden Cromwell, a guy in my depart-ment. This has been happening over a period of years. Someone from the WJR accounting department is probably part of the scheme, but that's not the issue now.

The evidence seems irrefutable. There are copies of WJR invoices to the phantom company and deposit slips for Cromwell. The client letter demands an explanation from you and a restitution of $500,000 by check within three working days or the agency will lose the account immediately and a lawsuit will be forthcoming.

Allie had taken the client's letter and directly confronted Vandy. Even though caught red-handed, Cromwell vehemently denied everything and vaguely mumbled something about his own lawsuit. This was becoming way too much for Allie, and he could no longer withhold the information from his boss. Knowing Norman was tied up in a new business presentation, he sent his GM an email.

He had dreaded sending the information. But the worst was yet to come. Facing Norman.

LOS ANGELES, 8:30 A.M.

Marcy burst through the double glass doors into the WJR/LA lobby, which was furnished in an identical manner to that of Chicago and New York. The same luxurious blue leather, over-stuffed chairs, the same deep blue carpet. Will's idea—no matter which WJR office you entered, you felt it was familiar territory. She moved quickly toward her office before anyone could intercept her with questions about the future of WJR Advertising. Her long-time secretary and part-time confidant, Ethel, followed her through the door, and then closed it, clutching a handful of messages. Marcy liked Ethel to take the messages off the voice mail and write them down the old fashioned way so that the agency head could sort them into the order in which she wanted to handle them. Marcy hated voice mail. It was hard to reach some people because they used it to screen calls, never answering the phone. The other thing that irritated her was phone tag–after several callbacks and listening to additional detailed messages, it was hard to remember whom you had actually talked to and who had simply left a message.

"Hi," greeted Ethel. "You've got Myra all over your back–she's called twice."

"She probably wants to know what's going on in the company."

"And whether you have any kind of a chance at the big job," added Ethel.

"Anything in her column today?"

"Just the usual gossip and garbage," replied Ethel.

"Who else wants a piece of me?"

"Eric Hanson called about the demise of the leader." Ethel suddenly grew hesitant.

"My gosh, you do know about Will, right?"

Marcy acknowledged with a hand wave.

"Terrible, isn't it? I always liked him," Marcy said somberly.

"Anyway, Hanson said there might be a Board meeting coming up real soon. He'll call back."

"A board meeting? How soon? What for?"

"He didn't say. There's also a delegation from the creative department that wants to show you the latest on Caesar's."

"Do they act like they really have something?" asked Marcy apprehensively.

"Yeah, but they did the last three times, too."

"I'm not ready for them quite yet. A little later. So what else do you have?"

"Just the usual collection of job applicants, personal stuff, stock brokers and such," said Ethel handing her the rest of the pink slips.

Her assistant turned to leave, then stopped and turned back toward Marcy. "You know, it might be a good idea to have an agency meeting to tell everyone what's going on."

"Ethel, baby, I don't have a clue about what's going on."

"You'll think of something. What time do you want the meeting?" asked Ethel, on her way out.

"Four o'clock would be okay," replied Marcy with a smile. That would give her the day.

"Do you want me to call the other offices and find out what they're doing and what's going on with funeral arrangements, client announcements and such?"

"Good idea."

As Ethel reached the doorway, she stopped and turned again toward Marcy. "You're not moving to Chicago or New York, are you?"

"I don't think so," mused Marcy. "I'm still the new kid on the block. Besides, most of the agency's business is east of the Rockies. Norman and Miller have the power bases. There will be some kind of a vote. I think I'll be staying right here in LA."

"Hope you're right. I couldn't possibly train another boss," said Ethel, this time exiting for good and closing the door softly behind her so Marcy could take care of her calls in private.

What a treasure Ethel was. Like Marcy, she was a tall, leggy blonde with great style and great instincts. She possessed a rare combination of organizational smarts along with the tact to handle all the people who were next to, or wanted to get next to Marcy. When Marcy was out of the office, no matter what your title in WJR/LA, everything went through her assistant.

Ethel also had a sixth sense about when to be Marcy's executive assistant and when to be her confidant.

Marcy kicked off her shoes, rested her legs on the white marble desktop and leaned back in her black leather chair, accented in chrome. Everything in the office was elegantly done in black and white. It was Marcy's idea. The black and white scheme created a backdrop for her. In this setting Marcy provided all the color.

Today Marcy's ensemble was a double-breasted blue pinstriped suit from LaScada worn over a white tee shirt from the Gap. She had the knack of combining designer clothes and everyday garb to create a statement. Today's statement was painful to make, but necessary. "Don't forget who's in charge here. Even though the Big Buddha is gone, don't worry. We'll be okay. And we've still got a business to run here in LA."

She picked up her messages and arranged them in descending order. Better not call Myra before I talk to Norman or Eric. Whatever I tell her will probably be the lead in Friday's column.

Marcy called Ethel to contact MJ, the creative director, to assemble the troops for the Caesar's creative show and tell. She had decided to review the new campaigns in the creative conference room, to help put the creatives at ease in their own lair. They were already intimidated enough by everything that had happened.

Taking off her jacket and tossing it over her shoulder, she swept into the conference room. "So, what do you have, hot shots?" asked Marcy, forcing her warmest smile.

She was not optimistic.

WHITE SULPHUR SPRINGS, 11:45 A.M.

Back in his hotel room, Eric stood up so he could stretch out his legs to soothe his aching knee. He had a yellow pad and pencil, and was now prepared to get his thoughts together.

"What needs to be done first?" asked Sadie.

"Get the word out to all the troops, I suppose," answered Eric, beginning to scribble on the pad.

"I don't think so," countered Sadie. "You've already got in touch with the GM's. The word is already out. Besides, it's on the internet and in the press. It's everywhere."

"Deal with the funeral? I should say a few words."

"Why not let the family handle all the arrangements and such. As soon as they track down Emily in the shops along Michigan Avenue, she'll probably take over all the personal arrangements."

Eric raised his eyebrows and glanced at Sadie, a signal that the "shops" comment was uncalled for. Emily Raffensberger and Sadie never did get along.

"What are you thinking?" asked Eric.

"Don't waste your time doing what someone else can or will do anyway. The most important thing you need to orchestrate," said Sadie, now in command, "is the selection of the new CEO. You."

"Yep. Sounds like you have an idea," said Eric.

"Let's see where you stand," Sadie added. "Why not make a list of the board members and the votes."

"Okay," answered Eric, warming to the task.

He put together three columns on his yellow pad. "Let me think this through a minute."

Board Member	Vote For	Action
Hanson	Hanson	–
Steinberg	Steinberg	Forget it
Gallipo	Don't know	Give it a try
Miller	Hanson, good chance	Get to him fast
Bunker	Hanson probably	Must get to him
Arness	Hanson hopefully, but don't really know	Find out, but he's out of the country

He handed the pad to Sadie. For the first time, Eric felt positive about his prospects. Obviously, each of the three general managers had an ax to grind. But why wouldn't he be the ultimate compromise candidate? At least the choice of Andrew and Marcy. And if he had three of the six votes, at least he couldn't lose.

"Who's Arness," asked Sadie.

"A management consultant who Will liked."

"So you don't know whose side he's on."

"No, but I think I should call a board meeting soon," he said en-thusiastically.

"As I remember, Arness is out of the country—I need to get in touch with him first. I think there's a two-day notice for a board meeting in the by-laws. If I catch up with him now, I can comply with the time frame and maybe have the board meeting by Sunday in Chicago. It would be nice to get this over with. If it's done quickly, maybe no one else will have a chance to organize any opposition."

"Let's think about the vote," replied Sadie thoughtfully, as she studied the sheet. "Everyone's vote is equal."

"Right."

"And all you—or anyone needs—is a simple majority."

"Right."

"So you have the Norwegian vote: yours," said Sadie in a rare at-tempt at humor. "And you can probably get Bunker. I mean he hardly knows the others and it's likely he figures you would be the best bet to keep the company together. And I agree you can probably get Andrew. I think he's always liked you and he's always been a company man. So if you get Bunker and Miller, you have three out of six, with Norman against you and Marcy and Arness undecided. Now, how does this majority situation work?"

"I don't know. I've never thought about it. Even after Will brought the office GM's on as directors, he still always had me and the two outside directors in his camp, so he always had a majority."

"How come he always had control of the outside directors? I thought outsiders on a board were supposed to be objective."

"Nope," laughed Eric mirthlessly. "Not on this board. Will is the one who put them on the board and decided to set the director's fee at $25,000. Twenty-five grand buys you a lot of loyalty. Besides, if any of the four of us were ever absent, Will voted their proxies. Hey, the GM's would never vote against Will anyway. Every vote was unanimous in his favor."

"But would the outside directors vote against you?" questioned Sadie.

"Maybe Arness," replied Eric, his newfound confidence draining somewhat.

"Let's get back to this hung jury situation. If you have your vote, Bunker and Miller, but not the other three, what will happen?"

"Well, it seems that I can't lose. And no one else can win. So somehow I need to get Arness or Marcy to come over. First I have to find Arness though. He's somewhere out of the country. With Arness here, maybe I can just out-wait the hung-vote situation until someone gives in."

"Possibly," said Sadie, "But what if you could avoid the three-to-three situation? It seems to me that the longer the boardroom politics go on, the better chance it gives someone else to form another coalition."

"I suppose that could happen," reflected Eric.

"Look. Let's say you get Bunker and Miller on your side. Then you call the board meeting, say for Sunday, but you *don't* try to find Arness. You should have a quorum. If he doesn't make the meeting, then you have it three to two. You're in."

"What about the by-laws? I have to notify him."

"The hell with the by-laws," exclaimed Sadie. "The moment you become CEO who's going to challenge you? Then you can change the stupid bylaws later."

"So forget about Arness?"

"Right."

"I need to thank about that," replied Eric. "Sounds like kind of a ruthless thing to do."

"What's to think about? It's not a crime or anything. Besides, if it's good for the company, it's not ruthless. Why not get a fax out Friday, announcing a Sunday board meeting. You meet the two-day requirement. So Arness, wherever he is, somehow doesn't get the fax. It happens."

Sadie had pushed him to the edge. Now Eric stepped over.

"Sounds like I've got to get to Bunker and Miller right away," he said.

Andrew stood, hands in pockets with shirt sleeves rolled up, in front of the window over-looking Michigan Avenue. He always thought better on his feet.

One of his first acts of the morning had been to email the staffers at WJR/Chicago with the news about Will. It had been a difficult memo to compose.

He walked over to his desk and picked up the ENNU file. An advertising sage once said, "The day you get an account is the day you begin to lose it." Sooner or later you'd be fired. The only question was whether it would be sooner or later.

There was no denying that the ENNU Footwear account was in trouble. WJR had won this most glamorous account three years ago, after a creative shoot-out against two of the giant multi-national agencies in Chicago. As the new client then exclaimed effusively in ad speak, it was WJR's superior strategic thinking that won the day.

The WJR strategy was unusual and unusually ballsy. It showed insight into ENNU's aggressive psyche, its entrepreneurial culture and the situation in the marketplace. ENNU was a young company up against entrenched competition and a dominant market leader.

WJR's strategic idea was "WATCH OUT NIKE."

By positioning the relatively unknown challenger against the leader, it gave the newcomer instant credibility in the market. One ad in the campaign was

"YOU WERE EXPECTING MAYBE NIKE?"

Still another was

"ENNU. WHAT'S REALLY NEW.
WATCH OUT NIKE."

WJR's problem now with ENNU was not the strategy or the creative executions. In fact, the ad campaign was working like crazy.

The "WATCH OUT NIKE." campaign had gotten this newcomer a hearing with both the distribution and the consumers. And the product had delivered. This pleased the three entrepreneurial founders—two guys who had worked for a plastics company and an accountant.

No, it wasn't the advertising or the company's performance that was WJR's problem. In the past six months the three entrepreneurs had been unable to cope with success and suffered a falling out. The accountant cashed out, leaving the plastic twosome. Instead of trying to duke it out, the two wisely agreed to hire a professional manager and brought in the president of a tennis company to run ENNU.

It appeared that WJR was now being victimized by this client management change. The situation was not unique to WJR. In fact, new blood at the top had become one of the leading causes ad agencies lost accounts in recent years.

Simon Slater, the new client president, apparently wanted his own people in charge, his own agency in the wings, and his own campaign filling the airways and the billboards around America. After being in the saddle only 10 days, Simon had written a letter to Andrew and as an introduction, stated he was in the process of reviewing everything ENNU did, including the advertising. He wanted to see some new thinking. The two presentations Andrew's creative team had made (without Simon in attendance) had resulted in no decisions. No one at the client wanted to commit, or even comment, until they knew what Simon thought. So far he had been "too busy" to sit in on the presentations.

It was a bizarre situation. The guy who wanted new work hadn't even seen it.

The immediate need was simple. Andrew had to get to Simon directly and quickly to confront him, so WJR could determine how to hang on to the account.

If he couldn't get a meeting with Simon, WJR was probably toast. And Andrew would be in a very vulnerable position in the post-Will WJR.

Edwin N. "Sandy" bunker ran his fingers through his hair, one of his nervous gestures that signaled concern.

Even though thinning sand-colored hair framed his rounded, pleasant face, the "Sandy" nickname was golf related. A lifelong player, Bunker possessed a dazzling short game. One of his prime skills was being able to blast the ball out from a greenside sand bunker close enough to the hole to one putt, commonly called a "sandy".

Returning to his office after a loan committee meeting, Bunker noticed a phone message from a Sir George Helmsley in London. The name didn't register. He did not return the call. Instead, he called his assistant, Oliver Stahlquist.

"Dig out the WJR file for me, Ollie."

"What's up?"

"Well, I assume you've heard about Will Raffensberger going down. It seems to be prudent to take a look at where they are on their loan and their line."

"You got it."

"Just leave it on my desk, please. I'll take a look at it after lunch," said Bunker. He didn't need the file to know that the WJR situation was a big problem. His loan officer on the account had kept him up-to-date, but now he wanted to know how big the problem was.

Sandy decided to lunch at the River Club rather than in the bank's executive dining room. The Club was one of the few places in town where you could lunch alone without feeling awkward. In fact, there was one corner of the grill where singles were customarily seated. On the other hand, if you were looking for company, you could be seated at a "Club" table for members who didn't have a lunch date, but didn't want to eat alone. Sandy also could have had a sandwich brought down from the bank's dining room, but today he wanted to get outside for a walk. Walking cleared his head and spawned some of his most productive ideas. And he might even want a cocktail while he thought through the WJR problem.

Heading out on LaSalle Street toward the river, Sandy considered the situation, breaking it down into two parts. Part one was WJR as the bank's current customer...WJR Today. The establishment of the WJR expanded line of credit three years ago was a borderline deal. Bunker had vouched for WJR and uncharacteristically he had even bullied the loan committee for approval. He had no idea why he had gone out on a limb for Will. The ad man was a charming devil though. At that time, as the newly anointed chief operating officer at the bank, Bunker's career was progressing very nicely. All he had to do was to keep his career on cruise control so he could put himself solidly in line for the CEO job, which would open up in only a few years. Bunker had been chosen COO over two other executive VP's. Perhaps his bravado in building up the WJR business was simply to show the two peers he left behind that the Old Boy had indeed selected the right successor. If this WJR thing got out of hand...and got out, those two would be nipping at his heels again in short order.

The WJR line of credit situation in Year One went along fine, but year two–last year–was a disaster. WJR lost several million dollars, seemingly due to a client suddenly declaring bankruptcy. WJR was forced to pay the bills to the magazine and television media, but the client in bankruptcy refused to reimburse WJR a large portion of the invoices to the tune of $2.5 million. While the problem was kept quiet on the advertising street, Bunker had known that the terrible year financially had dropped the WJR equity well below the bank's requirement.

If WJR went in the tank, there were no assets to attack, little to sell off. The bank would be left holding the bag. Bunker would be left holding the bag.

When Sandy learned of the problem last year, he knew that he should have restructured the line of credit immediately and forced

Will to pledge additional assets–personal–to cover the deficit in WJR's equity.

Once the 100% owner of WJR, over the years Will had rewarded his senior managers with shares of stock.

His holdings were now reduced to 72.6%. He was the one Bunker should have gone after. Now, however, because the WJR buy/sell agreement would force the company to buy back Will's shares within a year, the banker now had nowhere to turn. It was a mess.

"Hello, Mr. Bunker," smiled the doorman at the River Club.

"Hi, Bert."

Sandy walked under the gray stone Gothic arch with the "1879" etched in the middle. He passed through the ancient hand-carved door into the hallowed hallways of the club that rose from the Chicago fire ashes along the Chicago River. The pioneers who rebuilt the city built the stone club building on the riverbank. While the Club had been remodeled periodically over the years, the entrance and front door still remained from the original structure.

Sandy hung his raincoat in the cloakroom and turned into the adjacent main floor men's room. Almost every time he entered what must be one of Chicago's oldest and most elegant bathrooms, he remembered his father telling him as a youth, "Edwin, you must always stop and wash your hands when you enter a gentleman's club–whether you need to or not."

As the banker was seated by the captain at his customary dine-alone table, he decided that there was probably nothing he could do now about part one of the WJR problem–the current customer, "WJR Today". Perhaps there were personal assets from Will's estate (a distasteful thought) or the minority stockholders (unlikely) that could be contributed to the agency's balance sheet. Very messy.

However, part two, "WJR Tomorrow," where does the agency go from here, and who leads it, was another story to consider. As a director, Sandy felt compelled to be part of the solution, to have a big say in how WJR would be run and who would run it. He would have to help the agency through its financial crisis, which was becoming Bunker's potential personal crisis.

Satisfied with his thought process, Sandy decided he did not need to break his no-drinking-at-lunch rule after all.

"Iced tea, please," he asked the waiter.

Sandy had solved no problems, but at least he had crystallized his thinking. And he knew he could not sit on the sidelines and watch the WJR mess unfold.

He must be an active participant. The bank's money was at stake. Not to mention his career path.

NEW YORK, 1:00 P.M.

Norman had ensconced himself sat in a corner of his favorite luncheon haunt, Smith and Wolensky's. His well-manicured fingers cradled a glass of excellent Merlot. He was not much of a drinker and almost never indulged at lunch, either alone or with companions. Today was an exception.

Norman began writing on a piece of paper to organize his thoughts about the CEO job. There would be a board meeting. There would be a vote. The majority of the votes would determine who would become the new CEO of WJR. Simple. The next regularly scheduled board meeting was in two weeks.

Until Will's death last night, Norman had a single, highly focused strategy for ultimate success. Use his greatest talent—attracting new accounts—to grow WJR/New York and become the dominant WJR office in terms of revenue and prestige. Then when Will stepped down (whenever that was), Norman would be the obvious choice. Even it he weren't the people's choice; he believed he could make enough noise, if necessary, about his power and revenue base to swing things his way.

So far, the strategy was working. WJR/New York had become substantially larger than Chicago. Norman had already spent considerable time lobbying with Will to designate New York as the corporate headquarters. While Will had resisted, at least he had been listening and Norman had felt it would only be a matter of time. "You have to forget the sentimentality of Chicago, Will," he persisted. "Look, New York is where the action is in this business. If we're going to be a player in the future, we have to be around the action."

"Another wine, sir?" asked the waiter.

"No thanks, just give me the steak sandwich. Medium. Fries."

As the waiter retreated, Norman continued writing. Shortly, he put down his pen and reflected upon his treatise. He couldn't help smiling to himself at the headline he had written to identify his quest.

THE NORMAN CONQUEST

A perfect headline. Direct. Aggressive. Descriptive. Short and sweet. Underneath he had written:

> Three more votes.
> Gallipo!
> Miller?
> Arness?
> Bunker?

The "Norman Conquest" began with his own vote. He needed three more to gain a clear majority of four out of six.

The list was compiled in descending order of his confidence in attracting votes from directors. He had not even bothered to list Hanson, whom he detested, and referred to privately as "that napkin arranger." Besides, it was likely that Eric Hanson would assume that he should inherit the big job.

The first step was to get Marcy's support for his candidacy. She was the key to everything. If Marcy were on his side, just the two of them would control the lion's share of WJR's billings total.

He turned the paper over and wrote down the office-by-office billings breakdown.

NY	220
LA	90
Chicago	<u>170</u>
	480

So, together he and Marcy would control $310 million of the $480 total. Powerful. Two-thirds of the business.

When Norman and Marcy were aligned–East coast and West coast–symbolically Andrew would be surrounded and outnumbered. With Marcy in his camp, Norman figured that he had a reasonably good chance of getting Andrew on board. Even though they were direct opposites in many ways, Norman admired Andrew's skills.

Norman believed that Andrew was one of a dying breed–the true company man. Someone who would do what's best for the company.

Norman also believed that Andrew respected the New Yorker's professional skills–his organizational talent and business-getting record. All in all, the two had gotten along okay. It was even possible that when Norman became CEO, they might even become friends.

If Norman had both Marcy and Andrew on his side, it was a slam-dunk. Both Bunker and Arness would "get it": the people who run the business–who <u>control</u> the business–have spoken. It was Economics 101. How could the outside directors not go along with Norman? Anyway, if he had Marcy and Andrew on his side he only needed one of the outsiders.

Norman made notes on the paper while he deliberated over the "Norman Conquest." In the worst case scenario, even if he couldn't persuade Andrew, he had a good shot at Arness. They got on well at WJR board meetings and the accompanying dinners. Then, with Arness on his side, Bunker would probably come over.

What about winning over Marcy? In Norman's mind that didn't seem overly difficult, unless she had some relationship he was not aware of. Could there be something going on with Eric Hanson? Or Andrew Miller? Very unlikely, he thought.

As his steak arrived, Norman folded up the "Norman Conquest" and placed it inside his coat pocket. The biggest pitch of his career was about to begin. He had less than two weeks to make it happen.

It all began with the conquest of Marcy. He thought he knew her pretty well, but you couldn't take anything for granted. The stakes were too high.

LONDON, 6:15 P.M.

The silver-haired man sipping tea in the lobby of the Connaught Hotel in London somehow balanced a pipe, a teacup and a newspaper. Suddenly, he put his teacup down on the saucer with a rattle and hurled his *Herald Tribune* violently down onto the elegant, but worn oriental carpet. Sir George Helmsley had just discovered the small article, almost buried on the lower right hand side of page four, that announced the untimely death of the American ad man, Will Raffensberger. His hand tightened perceptibly on his pipe. What bloody luck. Sir George and Will Raffensberger were only 48 hours from inking a pact to sell WJR to the giant British advertising agency, Helmsley and Hofer, headed by the man in the hotel lobby.

If Will's airline ticket jacket would somehow have been found in the charred wreckage of flight 1031, it would have shown a return ticket from Roanoke to Washington, D.C., where Will would board a plane for London. Will had no doubt that Eric and the outside directors would endorse the WJR sale.

A handsome man with precisely trimmed silver mustache to match his wavy, neatly combed hair, Helmsley, from the neck down, was another story. Sir George was a rumpled figure that even a tailored, expensive suit and striped Turnbull & Asser shirt couldn't hide. Although blessed with an extremely neat mind, he somehow made a custom Savile Row suit look like an off the rack job. In all other ways, however, he was a proper gentleman, with the exception of the current outburst connected to the newspaper article. Signaling the waiter to deliver a single malt scotch, he picked up the newspaper and pondered the impact of its contents.

His global expansion plans into the U.S. were now dashed. WJR would have been a perfect union, and the price was right. His cash infusion into the American agency would have provided the cash flow that would dramatically reduce the amount now on the U.S. company's line of credit, and WJR would have been rescued financially.

"Damn it all," exclaimed the agency leader.

"Beg pardon, sir?" replied the waiter returning with his scotch.

"Not you, man."

"Thank you very much, sir."

Calming down a bit as he sipped on his scotch, Sir George wondered what could be done. He had problems of his own that the acquisition would have solved. He still had a letter of intent from Will. Was that binding in any way?

CHICAGO, 12:30 P.M.

Andrew somehow made it through a series of meetings, a flurry of phone calls, and several queries from in and out of the office about what would happen now in the post-Will future. Deflecting the Raffensberger queries with a "too early to tell" response, he spent most of his time speculating over the prospects of saving the ENNU account.

Andrew needed time to think, and he wanted desperately to get out of the office. He was tired of people asking him questions about the company's future, his future, their future. From everything he understood about human nature, he knew that every question really related directly to the person asking (What's this mean to me? What happens to my job?).

Andrew had no answers.

He buzzed June on his phone. "Who has the Cubbie tickets to-day?"

"Hugo Sotters has two, but there are two left," she answered.

"Who's he taking? Do you know?"

"I think he's taking one of his retired buddies from Glenview."

"Good, bring me the other two, please. I'm going out there for lunch."

Every once in awhile, maybe twice a season, Andrew would take a break at Wrigley Field. Playing hooky in Chicago to go watch the beloved Cubs from time-to-time was part of the rites of passage for every youngster growing up in the area. Andrew would drive or cab it to the park, have a hot dog and a beer and watch a few innings until his sanity came back enough to return to work. On occasion he wouldn't go back to the office. Wrigley Field was the perfect haven for Andrew because it was one of the few public places not invaded by the advertising business. Advertising signs and slogans weren't plastered everywhere inside the park or all over the outfield walls. Just the soothing, familiar vines along the outfield wall. Ivy. Blue sky. Sunshine. Out in the bleachers was a backdrop of white tee shirts mixed with the tanned bare-chested types and on warm sunny days, a plethora of halter-tops. In the box seats sat representatives of corporate Chicago in white shirts with sleeves rolled up and ties pulled down. Interspersed throughout were the youth of Chicago (the "yoots" of Chicago, as the senior Mayor Daley had affectionately called them.)

Andrew started stuffing his brief case with the contents of his IN basket, email printouts, memos, letters, magazines–just in case he didn't return. June walked in and handed him an envelope with the tickets.

"I moved your meeting with Whitey to tomorrow," she said, knowing that he might or might not be back.

"I've got my cell," Andrew replied.

"Don't worry. I won't call you unless you get a call from out of town."

"Or from ENNU," added Andrew.

"Of course, from ENNU."

Andrew opened the envelope and removed the two tickets, as June took the contents of his OUT basket.

Andrew put on his suit coat, straightened his tie, and assumed the air of someone who looked like he was on his way to somewhere important. Even though as the GM of the office, he could announce over loud speakers that he was going to watch the Cubbies and anyone who didn't like it could stuff it and start packing their bags, he still felt a pang of guilt. Andrew was an old school leader...the captain doesn't eat until the troops are fed...don't ask the troops to do anything you wouldn't do, and all that. With a spring in his step, he walked briskly out of his office, took a right turn at June's desk, and pushed through the glass doors etched with WJR and turned toward the elevators. Glancing at his watch, he noticed it was one o'clock on the nose. He would miss the opening pitch, but so what. He hailed a cab and headed for Wrigley Field.

In the cab Andrew decided he ought to try once more to connect with Eric. They had traded phone calls. Andrew dialed his cellular and finally they connected.

"Andrew, you've heard the news?" Without waiting for an answer, Eric pressed on. "Listen, there's going to be a board meeting this weekend, probably Sunday. I'll get to you with the details. Can you and Sally have dinner with Sadie and me on Saturday night?"

Andrew's heart skipped a beat. A board meeting? This Sunday? What did Eric want to discuss?

"I think it's important that we talk," continued Eric. "I've got some ideas about where we go from here. I want to talk to you about your future, too. You've always been one of my favorites," Eric said.

"Yeah sure, Eric," Andrew replied hesitantly. "I'm, uh, not exactly sure what Sally has on for Saturday night."

"This is important, Andrew," Eric said persistently.

"Sure. Okay. I'll talk to Sally."

"You pick the place and make the arrangements. Say, oh, seven o'clock?"

"I'll take care of it. Do you want to give me a hint about your direction?"

"No, it's too important to discuss over the phone," said Eric. "Listen, I've got to go. Just leave a message on my voice mail about the place for dinner."

How transparent can you be thought Andrew. This must be Eric's pitch for the big job.

At the game, Andrew found it difficult to concentrate on baseball. What to do about ENNU? And where exactly was Eric coming from?

LOS ANGELES, 11:30 A.M.

Marcy's eyes swept around the walls of the conference room once more. The television storyboards and ad layouts were grouped by campaign and pinned on the tan cork walls, anchored by an oak railing at waist height all the way around the room, except for the front wall, which was white and used for projecting images. The table was light oak, with at least seven coats of varnish. The floor was covered with a tiger stripped carpet, which Marcy had installed immediately after her promotion to general manager. The room had pizzazz and style and energy. It was a great environment for selling.

Marcy was elated. The L.A. creative teams had come up with two excellent ideas. Their progress was particularly exciting considering all the struggles to date. Somehow MJ had broken the logjam and several new approaches came tumbling out. One of the approaches was right on for positioning the basic Caesar's restaurant chip product line. The second best idea would also be an effective campaign, but happily, with some changes here and there it could be adapted to function as the Blue Corn Chip new product introduction. It was Marcy's idea to salvage the second restaurant chip campaign and use it for the Blue Chips. It was a huge idea, and when Marcy suggested it, the tiger-striped room heaved a collective sigh of relief. Several of the creative staffers praised her. It was genuine.

"That's why I get the big bucks, my dears," she announced in characteristic Marcy fashion, as she left the meeting. "Nice going, all of you. Now, let's get it all ready for Monday," she said with a big smile and a wave.

Marcy stopped off at Ethel's office. "Please get a call into Raul. Of course, I'll talk to him if you can run him down. But if not, let him know we'll show him the basic campaign and the Blue Chip introduction on Monday. That will blow his rocks. Also, see if he has a preference for our dinner."

"Noo Yawk Norman called. Wants you to return it soonest. Says it's urgent," said Ethel.

"Shit, everything is urgent," replied Marcy.

Back at her desk, Marcy shuffled through her messages. There was another one from Norman. She guessed it related to Norman's candidacy for the top job. He didn't waste any time.

Marcy really didn't want to be in the middle of all this. In fact, maybe this was the time for her to think seriously about moving elsewhere. Over the years, she had received offers from other agencies to come over (and bring Raul's business with her). She also had one or two dip-your-toe-in conversations with Raul himself about possibly setting up an in-house agency with him. Now that she knew the Caesar's creative was going to be okay, she was ready to negotiate with Norman. Or even with Raul. Or anyone else who might come along. She called out to Ethel to get Norman on the phone at about 1:30, after lunch. Right now, Norman needed her more than she needed him.

He could wait.

KONA COAST, HAWAII, 9:00 A.M.

Decked out in a wildly flowered Hawaiian swimsuit/shirt combo, newly purchased from the hotel shop, Leon Arness stepped out of his room at the Mauna Kea hotel with his wife, Diana. He had just checked his messages and was relieved to see that the red message light was not flashing. Because it was already two o'clock in Chicago and an hour later in New York, Leon knew that the odds were good that the rest of the day on the Big Island was almost certain to be message free.

A principal with the management-consulting firm of Padgett, Pryor and Arness, Leon had a lot of irons in the fire. For once, however, he wanted to really get away from it all, and he had made it a point to contact all of his major clients to warn them he would be difficult to reach for several days. In fact, Leon had talked to Will just last Tuesday. Will had suggested something big might be in the wind, but it would wait until Leon's return.

Will and WJR were very small clients of Leon's firm. Although they were classmates at Yale, the two men were not really close. In fact, the advertising man rarely solicited Leon's advice. Leon realized that his primary relationship with WJR was as an outside director. And a rubber stamp director at that. Will's $25,000 annual directors fee was a nice stipend, and the business discussions at WJR board meetings were not terribly taxing to Leon.

The WJR arrangement and respite were very acceptable to Leon; the management consulting business was tough enough. It wasn't the consulting part. After you scrubbed down the client situation, figuring out how to counsel a client was relatively easy. It was the constant travel and the time-consuming interviewing of client personnel that took its toll on mind and body.

Leon was surprised at his need to get completely away from it all. It made him laugh at this solution—more travel to escape all the travel. Even if it was illogical, so far their trip to Hawaii was the perfect antidote to the rest of his life.

It was a blue bird day, the third of their well-earned vacation, and the couple headed for their favorite location at the beach, between the thatched bar and the water. Today they planned to read on their beach chairs, take a walk or two, and enjoy lunch out. In the afternoon, hit the pool once or twice, probably walk some more, and end up at the beach bar. A quiet dinner by the sea would cap the day.

Aaah, life was good. What the hell was he working so hard for when he could be enjoying more of this? The rationalization always was that he had to really hump on the job to be able to afford times like this. Leon knew that there was no slowing down, but for now at least he was going to ratchet back and savor the rest of their time on the Big Island.

For once, not a thing to worry about.

NEW YORK, 2:45 P.M.

Back in his office, Norman checked his email. Finally he got to the message from Allie Lombardi. Shit. He emailed back a two word answer, "HERE. NOW."

Allie almost tip toed into Norman's office, and when the boss waved him to a seat, he perched lightly on the edge of the chair and leaned forward earnestly. After going over the details of Vandy's transgression, a depressed Norman leaned back in his chair to think. Allie continued to sit straight up on the front edge of his chair. Norman made no move or comment to make it easy for his subordinate—this had all happened on his watch. What timing. How could that little turd steal that much money? Norman wondered. The money WJR/NY was going to have to cough up was bad enough(not like it's sitting around in petty cash) but Norman somehow was going to have to keep this affair under the radar, at least for the time being. Obviously, the problem would reflect badly on WJR/NY management. That would be Norman. Paying out $500,000 now was painful in itself. Even worse, the account was worth $2,000,000 a year in revenue to WJR.

He dismissed Allie with a disdainful wave of his arm, cautioning (threatening) him through clenched teeth to keep everything quiet for the next few days. Then he picked up the phone to summon Chet Weaver,the First Affiliated account director.

"Listen, the first thing you do is apologize. Then tell him I'm out of town but will visit him personally next week." Weaver nodded meekly. "Tell him restitution will be made immediately. You will hand-deliver a check to the client's office on Monday." Weaver continued to nod dutifully. "You don't even want to think about what will happen if word of this gets out before I get to the client." Weaver was now doing a bobble-head imitation.

Although Norman noted that a copy of the client's letter was sent to Will, now there was no one at the other end to read it. Lucky. He wondered...was it possible to keep the entire incident quiet, at least for a time? How am I going to cut a check for 500 K and keep it quiet? This would take some doing.

WHITE SULPHUR SPRINGS, 3:00 P.M.

Eric had placed a call to Will's wife...widow. He had no agenda, but felt the need to pass along his condolences, offer his help and suggest he was available to do a eulogy. All he got was the voice mail. She must be out somewhere handling the arrangements. Relieved, he left a lengthy message and went back to packing for home, leaving some clothing items out for the evening cocktail party at the 4A's.

Eric had wanted to get on a plane, *any* plane it seemed to Sadie, and head for one of the WJR offices. Sadie had dissuaded him.

"You don't want to go to New York. Seeing Norman is a waste of time. LA is too far, and doesn't fit your plan anyway. Chicago is where you ought to be. It's where your office is. But there's no reason to rush off now. We'll go home tomorrow. Why don't you try to get cocktails with Bunker late on Friday? You have the dinner with the Millers on Saturday, and then you're ready for the board meeting Sunday. Relax. Everything will fall into place."

Sadie was right. Unable to reach Bunker, he left it to his secretary at WJR/ Chicago to arrange the meeting with the banker, as well as handle the other arrangements. Now faced with a fair amount of time before cocktails, Eric reclined on his favorite chair in the room with the ottoman supporting his knee. He turned on the television and got a special, previewing the evening's semi-final NBA game. Eric liked watching basketball. The announcers were blah-blahing about home court advantage.

All that bullshit about "the crowd is getting into the game," annoyed Eric. The crowd couldn't play defense, the crowd couldn't shoot or rebound, the crowd couldn't do jack shit except yell.

He shifted his knee again and it reminded him of a basketball game of 40 years ago.

After leading the football team to an 8 and 2 slate and a tie for the conference championship, he and a six-foot, seven inch drink of water named Odett Richards led the Blair Red Devils to an 18 and 4 basketball record, advancing to the regional finals. Odett could go up and get the ball and he could score from in close.

Nine minutes into the regional final game, Eric crashed the boards after a missed jump shot and was knocked to the floor by a teammate who whiplashed his knee. As Eric came down, he heard a sharp pop in his left knee. He limped to the bench where he rubbed the knee and iced it down until half time. At that point, having overcome early game jitters (my God, there must be 1500 people out there), the Devils trailed by only a point, with Eric swishing five baskets and a pair of free throws. But, with Eric out, the team hit a dry spell and was down by nine points at half time.

During the half, while coach McCarney exhorted his charges to rebound and play defense, Eric gingerly walked back and forth testing his knee. He pronounced himself ready to go in the second half.

Although he played the entire second half, with the exception of a two-minute blow, Eric scored only three points and was obviously a step too slow on defense and afraid to really explode up to rebound effectively. The Devils lost by 18 and Eric climbed aboard the bus painfully.

In those days, if you hurt your knee in football or basketball, you simply rested the offending limb until it healed enough to play. Arthroscopic surgery was not an option and major surgery was a major decision. Obviously, there were few knee operations sponsored by high schools, particularly in rural Wisconsin, and particularly after the major sports season was over.

After a couple of days, the pain subsided somewhat, and begin to heal. But it was never quite the same and the pain came and went. The gimpy knee precluded his playing baseball in the spring. And that is how Eric discovered girls and journalism (where the girls were). The spring j-class took care of his final elective.

Eric went on to Wisconsin, majored in journalism with a minor in advertising. He made the varsity squad in basketball, but was the perennial seventh or eighth man.

As his sports career faded into the background, he turned his attention towards his journalism major. Upon graduation he was able to get a job in the advertising department of a farm implement company in Milwaukee, Wisconsin. There he met Sadie, the raven-haired pretty and sophisticated daughter of a foreman at the brewery. Sadie was enthralled by the handsome blonde star athlete. She just knew he was going places. Eric was her ticket out of Milwaukee to the bright lights, restaurants and shops of Chicago—a move she talked about constantly. They were engaged nine months after meeting, and married just nine months later. Sadie was interested in his career and was supportive, offering advice every step of the way.

Successful in his first job, he rose to advertising manager in three years. That was when he met Will, when his boss to be came to Milwaukee to pitch Eric's advertising account.

Eric's reverie was interrupted by the telephone, which Sadie answered.

"Who? With what company? Oh. Yes, he is here, but he's in the shower."

"Hey!" exclaimed Eric, gesturing to pass him the phone.

Sadie raised her finger to her mouth in the universal "shush" signal. "Can he call you back in ten minutes? Good. I have a pencil."

As she hung up, Eric still agitated asked, "Who was that?"

"Nelson Ripple from the *Times*. He wants to know what's going to happen at WJR. You didn't really want to take that call without thinking it through, did you?"

"No, I guess you're right. I wonder what I ought to tell him?"

"Not the truth, that's for sure. I think you ought to somehow have him feel that there's no problem, that there's a succession plan and that there will be a board meeting sometime next week. Maybe tell him right now you're really overcome with the personal loss and there's no urgency to deal with company matters. You know, I've been thinking. There's one other thing you should do."

"What's that?"

"Go into the office in Chicago and check out the by-laws. You'll at least know something the others don't."

"Right."

Eric made a note of it and then began rehearsing the conversation in his mind before calling the most widely read advertising columnist in the country. "The Ripple Effect" was required reading in the industry. He had to return the call. The guy would be at cocktails that night. Eric dialed the number with a sweaty hand.

CHICAGO, 2:10 P.M.

As Sandy Bunker returned to his office, he found the WJR file on his desk, as well as a note from his secretary with Eric Hanson's request to meet for cocktails at the Guild Club late Friday. Although he did not know Eric well–his dealings were with Will and WJR's CFO–this could be a good opportunity to find out what was going on with the company and what the options were for its leadership from here on out.

The note also curiously asked if he would be in town this week-end, but there was no explanation of the question.

Sandy voice mailed his now absent secretary "Yes, I'm on for cocktails tomorrow and yes, I'm in town for the weekend."

Normally, one of the more upbeat people around, the banker was depressed. The WJR account had become a black cloud over his life. Extending the line of credit in that situation was neither illegal nor immoral. It was simply bad business judgment on the banker's part. It was uncharacteristic of the self-described, cautious banker. He simply couldn't suppress a certain amount of resentment toward Will. It wasn't so much the numbers, it was that the ad man had made him feel like a patsy. He picked up the file and headed for his burgundy leather chair. Although he had worked in several offices in the bank, the 13-year-old chair moved with him. It had survived the disapproving scowls of several designers charged with updating his office decor. Somehow, he felt comfortable and in control in the shapeless overstuffed piece of furniture.

He opened the WJR file with a frown on his face. This would not be good reading.

NEW YORK, 4:25 P.M.

After touring the agency to follow-up his email about Will, now back in his office, an impatient Norman waited for Marcy to call. He rehearsed his conversation with her one more time.

He had decided to promise her the presidency of WJR. Will had been chairman, president and CEO. It was a large, almost unwieldy collection of titles, but when you own the joint, why not? It was clear who was in charge.

Now everything had changed. The chairman title was important, but it was the CEO designation that carried the weight. Norman would be chairman, CEO and run everything out of New York. Making Marcy president seemed to have a certain sense of symmetry–east coast/west coast. But he couldn't elevate Marcy without finding the right title for Andrew. Maybe Andrew should be president and Marcy could be vice chairman. Or should that be chairwoman? Chairperson?

Norman had decided to stick with the president title for Marcy. He *had* to get her on board first. In fact, maybe he should make her president/creative director of the entire company. Nah, probably not. The New York creative department would never stand for it. She would have to be satisfied with president. Not bad.

Maybe Andrew would be okay with the vice chairman title, he, Norman, would create. Vice chairman was a good "suit" title—an account service position. Initially, maybe Norman could convince both Andrew and Marcy separately that each was, in effect, the number two person in the company.

The architect of the "Norman Conquest" smiled. This could all work. First Marcy in my corner. She ought to jump at the president title. Next he would work on Miller and later get to Arness and Bunker.

Norman wondered when the board meeting would be. Who calls the board meeting now? Norman had no idea. But first things first. He had made some notes to guide his phone conversations with both Marcy and Andrew.

The phone rang. It was Marcy.

OAK PARK, ILLINOIS, 3:30 P.M.

After the initial shock, Emily Raffensberger was holding up as well as could be expected. Amidst the grief, the most immediate problem she faced was, as yet, there were no identified remains to bury. The funeral director gently suggested a memorial service. Emily agreed easily and decided that the service should be small and limited to family, friends and close business associates. Perhaps later there would be something larger that would include a wider range of acquaintances and the advertising community.

The services were scheduled for Sunday afternoon in the church chapel. Two of her three daughters were already with her and would be an enormous help in contacting friends and making arrangements. The three women decided there should be a get together after the services at the Raffensberger's rambling old home in suburban Oak Park.

Having dealt with some of the logistics, Emily felt a sense of panic. How would she pay for all this? She must get in touch with Will's financial planner. There were other questions that crossed her mind. Was she now the owner of WJR? Did she have to do anything about the company? Who could tell her? It was probably sensible to call one of the outside directors, The banker would seem to be the better choice. Didn't he know about money and things of that nature?

LOS ANGELES, 2:45 P.M.

Hanging up the phone after her conversation with Norman, Marcy rose from her desk and walked out to Ethel's alcove. She felt giddy, almost light headed.

"Hold my calls, babe. I need some quiet time." She wanted to contemplate Norman's proposal about the presidency. Relaxing on her sofa, she sifted through Norman's concept. It had really surprised her. Was this good? Was it too good to be true? What's wrong with this picture?

So she supports Norman and becomes president. That had a nice ring to it, she thought. It would be great to carry that title when she was in new business pitches. So what else would it mean? Would everyone in the company report to me? That might be difficult to orchestrate. She hadn't asked and Norman hadn't offered. This wasn't just a ceremonial thing, was it?

Norman's basic concept made sense to her. He's bright. We can't let that klutz Hanson sit in the big chair, she thought. Norman was the obvious alternative; he had the big numbers in New York. She knew for a fact that Norman had been on a crusade to move the headquarters to New York.

Maybe Andrew would go for the vice chairman title. Norman wanted her to help bring Andrew around. Why not. It was time the people actually running the business ran the business. Andrew would buy into that. But we still need one of the outside directors on board to make up a majority for Norman. Well, that was up to Norman.

NEW YORK, 6:35 P.M.

Back in his co-op, which was normally neat as a pin, Norman had gone from the front door directly to his bed, where he now lay spread eagled, staring at the ceiling. What a day. His almost non-stop presenting and planning had wiped him out. Fortunately, he had an hour or so to himself to wind down before it was time to venture out for the evening.

Tonight at the Big Apple A Day Cancer Charity event there would probably be a few questions to field. It was a black tie event, one of more than two dozen which Norman attended each year.

After a few minutes rest and a hot shower Norman was refreshed. Once again he was ready to take on the world. Tonight Norman would be working the room among New York's upper crust. There might be clients there to be schmoozed, and new business prospects with whom a beachhead might be established. Long-divorced, Norman would be able to move easily about the event without being encumbered by a wife.

He was one of the few men who actually liked to attend formal affairs. Not only was Norman a handsome, dashing figure in formal wear, he was also quite comfortable in it. Whistling, he expertly tied his black tie, remembering his father's admonishment when he was a youth, "A gentleman only ties his tie once, and then lives with the result."

Slipping on his jacket, he admired himself in the mirror, striking a variety of poses, ranging from head down with eyes narrowed and arms folded...to glancing over his right shoulder with a slightly quizzical expression. He should probably get a new photo taken to use for press releases. Having checked his image in the mirror from several angles, Norman was satisfied. The next CEO of WJR looked the part.

CHICAGO, 6:30 P.M.

Although Andrew boarded the 6:35 train with only a minute or so to spare, there were still seats available. The leather-jacketed Reebok-shod traders were home well before five and already tooling around in their BMW Seven Series or overseeing soccer practice, or figuring their current net worth on the home computer. The bankers, bridge-players and other nine-to-fivers had caught the 5:15 or 5:25.

Most everyone on the 6:35 looked like they had been through the ringer. Suit jackets that were folded and placed carefully on the overhead rack in the morning, were tossed in a heap up on that same rack now. Button down shirts were unbuttoned and ties were generally riding at half-mast. As a group, the train riders were a tired bunch hoping the plumbing hadn't crapped out at home, or one of the kids hadn't flunked a math test and needed aid and comfort. Most of them wanted simply to reach home base to dive into their drink of choice with no problems, no issues to face.

Andrew had just enough time to grab a shooter–a double vodka rocks, two olives. Maybe tomorrow he would cut back.. Tonight he needed a man-sized drink.

On the days that he took the train in the evening, Andrew tried to avoid acquaintances from either business or his North Shore community.

He was tired of the greetings "How's the ad game, Andy?"

Andrew felt obligated to keep coming up with different answers to the ad game question,

"We're winning six to five."

"It's better than doing five to 10 in Folsum prison."

"Hey, where else can you actually get paid to sit around and think things up and don't have to act like a grown up?"

If he felt particularly nasty, he might shoot back, "A lot more fun than the (fill in questioner's occupation) game."

Sometimes he just smiled weakly, and arched his eyebrows.

As the Northbound train lurched ahead, Andrew balanced himself as he once did on a rolling destroyer deck and squirmed out of his jacket. Tossing it casually on the rack, he burrowed down in his seat and reflected on the day. It was one of the worst days of his business life. His big boss died tragically and his biggest account was in deep shit. Tomorrow probably wasn't going to be any better. He raised the vodka rocks to his lips and inhaled.

He forgot about ENNU and began to wonder about the WJR succession, something he hadn't thought about in a long time. Over the years he had felt good about his chances down the road and was in no particular hurry. In conversations with Will Andrew was led to believe that he was at least one of the two prime candidates and the implication was that there was a reasonably good chance Will would swing the vote his way upon retirement. Chicago had always been the cradle and the soul of WJR and Will could have been sure that Andrew would keep it that way.

Andrew thought about what it would be like to be The Big Guy. Day to day it probably wouldn't be too much different than running the Chicago operation. More than once he had told Laura Forbes: "At any point in time, 15% of our people are unhappy and 15% of our clients are, too. My job is to find the disenchanted in each segment and then fix the problems. Simple."

Running all of WJR would mean he would worry about 15% of a larger pie of both people and clients. It was important to keep your people happy. In the agency business it usually wasn't their bosses who took you out, it was the people who worked for you. The troops found a way to leak the news to the board that so and so didn't have a clue how to manage them or the business. Once the leaks started, it was only a matter of time.

Andrew had returned to the office after the 7th inning. The Cubs were getting trounced by the New York Mets and he wanted to avoid the post-game traffic anyway. Returning to the office, he found messages from Eric and Norman. Both marked urgent.

The conversation with Norman was strained. Obviously, the New Yorker who was normally velvety smooth was somewhat uncomfortable in his self-coronation role and also in soliciting Andrew. Vice chairman? Was it a real job? It was hard to figure out. Andrew tried to think of other vice chairman he knew. He couldn't think of any.

During the conversation, Norman kept returning to the point that now with Will gone, it was up to the operating heads to run the business. Together they would keep WJR on track. They were a team. They were the future, with Norman holding the CEO title, and the other two GM's holding the other two important titles. No mention of Eric and his future. What if he, Andrew, agreed to fall in line with Norman, and later the New Yorker sacked him? Could he trust Norman? Probably not. On the other hand, working for Eric would be a circus.

Eric's call was non-committal, but there was mention about Andrew being the number two guy. Andrew's opinion of Eric was an empty suit. At least Norman was a skilled ad man.

One fact had become obvious to Andrew. Both Norman and Eric needed him. Both sides ostensibly wanted him to be the number two guy.

Am I better off with Norman or with Eric? Should I give up any chance for the top? If I do, I want something in return, he thought. Andrew was still not yet sure which candidate to support or what that something was as the train approached his stop.

One thing he knew for sure. They both needed him. As they say in Chicago, he had clout.

SANTA MONICA, 5:10 P.M.

Marcy pulled into the homeward-bound freeway with the happenings of the recent events running through her mind. God, what a day, she thought. This morning she woke up as the WJR west coast manager with one of her large accounts giving her fits. Tonight she was on her way to becoming (if all went well) president of WJR and the future prospects for the Caesar's account weren't looking all that bad.

Even the staff get-together went well. There were almost no questions and Marcy's assurance that LA would keep running as before was like a relaxant to the entire group. She kept it short and sweet—in a situation like this, the more you talked, the more people wanted to read into your comments the things that weren't there.

Now she was wiped. After a late night last night, it had been a non-stop day. But, some sort of celebration was in order. From the car she called LA Express, the one outfit that provided home delivery from some of the best restaurants in town. Marcy ordered their best champagne for her private celebration.

In the past couple of years Marcy had learned something important about being a general manager. Employees, clients and others, who didn't take you seriously as a creative director, hung on your every word as a GM. It almost didn't matter exactly what you said, it was how you said it. While there were frequent periods of self doubt, and an occasional feeling of total inadequacy (how did I ever think I could do this job?) the more she talked and acted like the GM, the more she grew into the role. Why shouldn't the same thing happen as president?

Wait a minute ... can't think about that now.

This president thing wasn't even for certain. And, of course, she wasn't home free yet with Raul. He could still dump on her two campaigns.

Friday

Sir George sat at the table in the morning room of his flat, pouring over a folder titled "Raffensberger." The newspaper article concerning Will's death was clipped on the front of the file.

The British advertising executive again reviewed his options regarding the WJR deal that were neatly printed on a piece of paper. The agreement had been with Will, who intended to run his company for three years while it was being integrated into the British company. Now, without Will, Sir George was forced to start over. The problems mounted. Could the deal be done? If so, who would run the acquired firm? With Will out of the picture, who's the contact? Sir George was a first things first kind of orchestrator. He reviewed his notes about the deal.

1. Forget doing a deal, any deal.

2. Look elsewhere for an acquisition in the U.S.
3. Use the letter of intent as a legal document and force the sale with the surviving owners (minority holders).
4. Convince the surviving owners that the deal still made sense financially—move ahead with their blessing.
5. Win the support of the outside directors and use their influ-ence to force the GM's to buy in.

Not doing a deal at all was not a good option. With the strong economy in the UK and the upsurge in Helmsley and Hofer stock, there was increasing pressure from H&H stockholders to make acquisitions. It was the only way to keep pace with other publicly traded agency stocks on the London stock exchange.

Option number two, to look elsewhere, was a problem. Having conducted an exhaustive search among U.S. privately held agencies over the last year, Sir. George felt that WJR was by far the best choice. The creative and business philosophies appeared to be similar to his company's, and there were no large conflicts—situations where competing clients would be thrown together under one agency banner. Besides, many of the large U.S. independents had already been snapped up. If WJR wouldn't work, he would be forced to start over, looking at the next tier of candidates. Not an appetizing thought.

Option number three, applying legal pressure, would probably not work. It would take too long; he was too far away physically. In addition, an unfriendly takeover in the advertising agency business was fraught with problems.

Option number four, selling the GM's and Hanson on the deal from ground zero did not look promising. At least in the short term. Convincing local managers of the need to go global would be difficult.

Option number five, winning support of the outside directors had some merit. At least it might be attractive to the banker on the board. Having studied the WJR financials supplied by Will, Sir George had knowledge of the severe financial problems facing WJR.

In fact, the financial situation was the basis of Will's willingness to talk when contacted by Helmsly. Sir George could handle the debt.

The Brit surmised that with Will gone, the financial morass would only worsen. Option five was indeed his best approach strategy. Enlist the outside directors, particularly Bunker, to force the issue and let them convince the general managers that the H&H deal was necessary to bail out WJR.

Satisfied that he had arrived at the best course of action, Sir George flipped through the WJR folder to find Bunker's bio and phone number.

He began making notes in preparation for a call to Chicago later in the day.

Bunker would become his ally and he, Sir George, would become the company's savior.

The question was, would he get a chance to state his case?

WINNETKA, 7:30 A.M.

Sally had picked up Andrew's Jaguar late Thursday. For once it was something minor like a fuse, a repair that didn't cost another $700.00, and Andrew was driving to work again.

As he cruised through the tree-framed streets in Winnetka, he thought back to his father's warning when he went into the agency business, "You go into advertising, you're asking for it. An agency gets into trouble, they fire people. They'll fire you. There are no manufacturing plants to sell, no mills to shut down. They have to fire the people. It's the only way to cut costs. Go to work for one of the blue chip companies. Get a job with IBM or Exxon, or someone like that."

The Old Man would turn over in his grave. IBM, Exxon, almost every major company had pruned itself back. In many cases, they had done it with a meat ax, sometimes firing 10,000 or 20,000 people at a time.

Was it possible that now the advertising business was more stable than the others? That's a laugh. Just when you thought everything was humming along—job going well, future bright, kids doing okay in school, little woman loving being a North Shore housewife—half your world turned to shit. First Will, then ENNU, what next? Another down cycle?

That was life. The only thing to do was to hang in there until the cycle turned upward again.

His typical commute took forty-five minutes because the stoplights along the route to Chicago were set so you traveled a steady pace no matter what month, day, or time it was. It was 45 minutes, never faster, and rarely slower. One thing in his life that was reasonably predictable.

It was true that when an agency lost a big account, the pink slips usually were not far behind. It was painful, but there was no choice. In fact, Andrew had always believed that this occasional forced exodus was, in the long run, healthy for an advertising agency, for any company. A survival-of-the-fittest proponent, Andrew endorsed the idea of periodically pruning out the dead wood. You had to do it to keep making the "nums."

Making the numbers, however, did not guarantee that you could relax and enjoy. If you made $10 million in profit one year, you were expected to make $12 million the next year. The crossbar went up inexorably. In some ways, success brought more pressure than failure. The more you grew your profit, the more the heavy breathers wanted and the more they wondered if you could do it again. And, the more closely they scrutinized your current plans and projected numbers.

As he turned into the parking lot underneath his building, his mind turned back to ENNU. He couldn't make the nums if he didn't hang on to this account!

Entering his offices, Andrew tossed his briefcase on the leather sofa and noticed there was a fax face down waiting for him on his desk. The Board meeting election announcement stunned him. Sure he had agreed to meet Eric for dinner tomorrow. But, after all, the WJR executive VP lived in the city and was due to come back to Chicago on Saturday anyway. Why did this succession thing have to be done so rapidly? A board meeting was coming up in, what, two weeks? What's the big hurry?

#

Fourteen blocks Southwest, a frowning Sandy Bunker studied the fax from Eric. What kind of a move was this anyway? Was it legal? Who had Eric consulted about this?

Reaching into one of his file drawers, Bunker pulled out his Director's copy of the WJR by-laws. Two minutes later he closed it up and returned it to the file. The CEO or president could call a Board meeting with 48 hours notice, either verbally or by written communication. The two-day rule was observed properly, but what about the CEO president thing? He guessed that Eric assumed he was acting president—part of his job description as EVP, in the absence of the president—and well within his rights to call a board meeting. Bunker resolved to find out what was going on when he met with Eric at cocktails.

As an outside director, he was going to flex his muscles. Besides, he had to look after his own interests.

NEW YORK, 9:40 A.M.

Norman arrived at the office uncharacteristically late. It had been a late night, but a nice way to unwind. There was a fax on his desk from Eric announcing that there would be a board meeting in Chicago on Sunday morning, and a memorial service for Will in the afternoon. The purpose of the board meeting, Eric explained, was to choose a new CEO and chairman.

Norman's mouth went dry. Certainly, he had not anticipated a meeting this soon. What the hell was Eric doing? What was he planning? There was a scheduled meeting coming up in two weeks, but moving it to Sunday...was it legal? What if he refused to attend? Nope, they could have a quorum without him. He had to show up or his candidacy had no chance. Could he delay the meeting? Didn't seem to be a way to do that.

Instead of having two weeks to execute the "Norman Conquest", he now had two days. Shit. Could he pull it off in such a short time frame?

So he had himself and Marcy, and maybe Andrew in his camp, although his conversation with the Chicagoan yesterday was inconclusive. Obviously, he needed Bunker or Arness, maybe both, and now he needed to move quickly. That was a problem. On the other hand, the rapid timing of the board meeting increased his chances of keeping the embezzlement thing under wraps. Norman's mood brightened. Maybe it was to his advantage after all. Hey, who was better at putting together a pitch in two days than he was?

Norman's voice mail was flashing. Impatiently he switched it on. He was flabbergasted to hear the message. It was from the heavyset executive from Associated Foods telling him that they were very impressed with yesterday's presentation. He went on to say that WJR had made the cut to the final four and they were in a hurry to move forward. They wanted to come back in next Tuesday. Norman returned the call immediately. Of course WJR/New York would be thrilled to meet with them again, answered Norman. The agency was eager to take the next step...what would they like to cover on Tuesday? After settling the details, Norman put down the phone with a broad smile.

"Unbelievable," he exclaimed out loud. "Fucking unbelievable." Go figure. The two of them didn't seem like they were interested at all, much less in a hurry. Now they wanted to come back early next week for the next step.

Norman pounded his desk in triumph. Made the cut! And looking good. Now he was heading to the definitive board meeting buoyed by the prospect of winning the largest account in WJR's history.

Suddenly, it seemed the timing of everything couldn't have been better for the New Yorker.

Now he just needed to keep this First Affiliated Bank thing under wraps.

LOS ANGELES, 9:00 A.M.

Marcy's day began with an interview with a prospective creative group head. Since the candidate had flown in the night before from San Francisco, there was no opportunity to change the meeting from what promised to be a wild day.

Thankfully, Clete Bubier was on time. Ethel ushered him in. Normally, Marcy went out to the lobby herself to greet visitors, but today she was busy sorting paperwork and tasks into the "must do today" file and the "wait until next week" folder. All the attention on the Caesar's problem had caused the work to stack up.

Tall with black curly hair, Bubier sauntered in confidently, wearing an off-white, loose fitting coat over a black t-shirt and black Calvin Klein jeans. Sporting the small, round, trendy wire rimmed glasses; he also featured the continuous three-day beard growth. He flashed a slightly crooked, but pleasant smile at Marcy.

She took an instant liking to him. That was good. Marcy believed that first impressions were extremely important in the agency business. Over the course of time, ad agency people would continually find themselves in new situations being introduced to new clients and new associates. Having the presence to start out on the right foot in every situation was important.

"Do they call you Clete?"

"Yep, it's short for Cletus...family name. There aren't too many nicknames that can come out of a name like mine."

"I guess not," she said warmly.

Marcy motioned him to a lounge chair in the grouping away from her desk.

"This black and white motif is pretty cool," said Clete. "Looks like I wore the right garb."

Marcy smiled again.

"I think you'll be more comfortable over here," she smiled, wondering whether Clete Bubier was a real talent or just another creative director who only looked the part.

"What would you like to know about me?" asked her visitor.

"Why don't we look at your book first," suggested Marcy.

"Fine. Would you like to just look or do you want the accompanying play by play?"

"Why don't you relax while I look," answered Marcy, as she began to page through his portfolio of samples. She was looking for powerful core ideas, not splashy design executions of ads. It seemed to her that there were fewer people nowadays who could really write. Too many of them were "television babies" who disguised a lack of ideas with colorful executions, jingles, T&A (tits and ass) beach scenes and the like.

Clete was an off-the-wall writer with an edgy style. In leafing through some of his early work for a small agency, she paused and grinned broadly. For a local car wash chain he attracted attention with two headlines:

"GET A HAND JOB. $11.95."

And

"BEST BLOW JOB IN TOWN. $11.95."

She wondered if the ads had really run. Some interviewees showed work that had never run. Some even showed work done primarily by someone else. Sometimes you saw work that the recruit had nothing to do with. You had to be careful.

"Did these ads really run?"

"Yeah, but not long, to tell the truth."

Ahhh, the truth was good. Clete was recommended by Marva Machey, probably the top creative recruiter on the West Coast. Marcy detested Marva and hated paying her the 30% of salary fee, but grudgingly admitted she knew where the talent was. Marcy also wanted to stay on her good side, with an assignment now and then. Otherwise the recruiter could raid her staff. .

Marcy paged past the television storyboards to examine the print samples. A great television spot director or an editor might save a lousy idea from a creative director. In her mind, ideas in the print medium were naked. One of her techniques was to read the headline, the first line of copy and then skip to the close. Most copywriters toiled over the headline and intro of an ad, but only the dedicated writers spent as much time writing the last line as the first.

"I remember this campaign, "said Marcy. "How did it work?"

It was a series of billboards for a popsicle type ice on a stick product. One simply showed the product with a crumpled wrapper and the headline,

"LA SUCKS."

Another was a similar visual with a headline,

"IN YOUR FACE SUCKAH."

"It was dynamite," answered the writer. "We really forced the distribution. Pushed the product on the shelves, then pulled it off. Business up 12% in six months."

Good answer. It was encouraging to find a creative person who related business results to his work. Clete was either a real talent or really well rehearsed.

After moving up to general manager of WJR, Marcy knew she had to back fill with one or two senior creative people to take up the slack. Some of the other work she had seen recently made her wonder if they still taught grammar in grade school, but Clete's stuff looked promising.

Now, if she promoted MJ to general manager—she was the obvious choice—someone would have to take over as creative director. There were two candidates now in the shop. This Clete might be a third.

An ad for the children's department of one of LA's finest stores read,

"YOUR MOTHER WEARS ARMANI BOOTS."

"Clete, I like what I see. Now tell me what's wrong with you?"

He smiled. "Is that a trick question?"

"Absolutely," said Marcy, as she settled into her chair and prepared to find out what, if anything, was wrong with Clete Bubier.

Later in the discussion, Marcy interrupted with "How much do you make, Clete?"

He was somewhat flustered, and blurted out "One twenty five".

The unexpected interruption was one way Marcy got to the truth about how much money an applicant was earning. She never asked how much someone wanted. If you asked and then didn't give it to him, you were an asshole.

CHICAGO, 11:10 A.M.

Doodling on his yellow legal-sized pad, Sandy Bunker was trying to make sense of the WJR/CEO situation. He was scheduled to meet Eric at Hanson's club, the Guild Club at 5:15 that afternoon. Since this was Eric's meeting, that's when he would reveal his hand. By then, however, there wouldn't be much time before the board meeting to block a proposal by Eric. On the other hand, Bunker wasn't yet sure what he wanted to happen. Who were the CEO candidates and which one would do the best job in protecting the bank's position? Perhaps it was Eric. At least he had some seasoning. He was the number two guy. At least on paper. Maybe Sandy should give Arness a call to see what he was thinking.

His call to Arness resulted only in reaching Leon's voice mail.

Bunker's secretary flashed him. "It's someone named Sir George Helmsley from London." The name didn't register with Bunker.

"Did he give the name of the company?"

"No."

"Well, okay, I'll take it." You never knew when the stranger on the other end of the line was a prospect for the bank.

After introducing himself, Helmsley went through his story and his intentions. Bunker muffled his surprise at the proposed deal, and listened intently, asking questions throughout the conversation.

Probing for the financial details of the deal, he felt a surge of admiration for Will. It would have been a triumph for the CEO to add global capabilities while solving the WJR financial problems as well.

Without Will, though, could it still work?

"Sir George, your proposal may have great merit. However, there is a real issue here that is much closer to home. The board meeting to select the new CEO has been scheduled for Sunday at 10:00 a.m., Chicago time.

"What's the hurry?" probed the Brit.

"There are reasons," replied Bunker, who had no idea what they were. He had been unable to reach Eric, who had already checked out of the Greenbriar by the time Bunker received his fax.

Sandy's secretary entered briskly and put a note on his desk that Norman was holding.

"I'll call him back," he mouthed.

Returning to his phone call, Bunker suggested, "Perhaps it makes sense for you to appear at the board meeting to present your proposal. Don't consider this an official invitation yet–I am just thinking out loud." There is a possibility the Brit could become the bank's lifesaver for the WJR account, he thought.

"I may very well want to do just that," said Sir George. "Let me consider the possibility of crossing the pond for your meeting and call you back today. Perhaps you will then be disposed to offer me the proper invitation."

"That would be fine," answered Bunker. "Good bye, Sir George."

The banker needed to weigh the possibilities and decided to delay the return call to Norman.

His secretary was on the line with another call. It was Emily Raffensberger. Geez. What next?

"Emily, I'm extremely shocked and upset at your tragedy," he said consolingly. "Is there anything—anything at all—that I can help you with right now?"

"Thank you, Edwin. (She never called him Sandy.) "That's nice of you," she replied softly. "This is all very confusing for me and I don't know what to do. I'm looking over some of Will's affairs. I was wondering what happens to his stock in the company. Is there anything I need to know? Or do? Do I own WJR now?"

"No, I'm sorry, Emily. You don't," he replied gently. "Will put in what is called a buy/sell agreement long ago. Since this is a partnership, even though he owned the lion's share, the company is required to buy back shares–in this case from the estate."

"Oh, yes. I believe I do remember Will talking about that a long time ago. With everything that's going on it simply slipped my mind."

"How are you holding up, Emily?"

"Pretty well, considering. The children are a big help in the arrangements."

"Good. If there's anything I can do please let me know."

"Thank you, Edwin."

"I'll see you Sunday then."

He had forgotten all about Will's shares. When the chairman first began selling some of his shares to WJR people, he established the buy/sell agreement to prevent the passing of those shares to a partner's estate. It was ironic that he was the first to be affected by the agreement.

ROANOKE, 12:15 P.M.

Eric and Sadie pushed ahead to the front of the line boarding flight 524 to Chicago. In changing their plans to return home two days early, Eric had paid a substantial amount to upgrade to first class, even though there were coach seats available. Although he frequently used miles to upgrade, at WJR you didn't buy first class seats unless you were Will, or were traveling with clients who had first class tickets. What the hell, thought Eric, the new CEO of WJR deserved to fly first cabin no matter what the circumstances. Will always did. Besides, Will was no longer around to scrutinize his expense report. Eric felt a sudden pang of guilt at these positive feelings because he no longer had to report to Will.

Earlier, as his last act before checking out of the hotel, Eric prepared a terse announcement of the WJR board meeting at 10:00 a.m. on Sunday, and faxed it to the three WJR GM's and to Sandy Bunker. No fax was sent to Leon Arness.

"So, how are you going to handle Bunker and Andrew?" asked Sadie.

"Well, neither one of them is going to be easy," answered Eric. "I figured I would just lay my case out on the table. You know that I'm the logical successor...and the one to keep the company together. I really think it's what Will would have wanted."

"I really wonder if they'll buy the 'Will wanted' stuff," said Sadie. "You need to have a stronger case."

LOS ANGELES, 9:30 A.M.

Ethel knocked lightly on the door before opening it to interrupt Marcy's interview with Clete. She delivered two important messages. One was the fax from Eric about the Board meeting.

"That's really fast," Marcy exclaimed. "I guess you'll have to get me on a plane tomorrow afternoon. I'll stay at the Drake, all the usual arrangements."

"Raul called. Wants to do your dinner tonight," said Ethel.

Marcy's first inclination was to put it off, but reconsidered. There was nothing going on until she had to leave for Chicago. This could be a good opportunity to pre-sell the two new campaigns...now that she was confident she had two campaigns to sell.

"Okay. Let me know when and where."

"One more call," said Ethel. "Bob Treadman wants to set up dinner, too."

"Not a chance," answered Marcy. "Once was enough. Call him and tell him I'm leaving town tomorrow for an extended period."

Clete sensed that the interview was over.

CHICAGO, 12:30 P.M.

Andrew was not looking forward to his lunch with Kimberly Johnson. But she had been persistent in trying to schedule the meeting and Andrew had agreed last week to today's lunch. Kim was a space salesperson, the Midwest Manager, of Action Sports, a weekly magazine that was carrying a heavy schedule of ENNU ads. Kimberly's agenda was to try to keep the schedule of advertising going in her publication. On the other hand, Andrew was searching for information about ENNU and perhaps Simon.

Space and time salespeople sold advertising space in magazines and newspapers, and time on radio and television, respectively. The veterans called themselves peddlers—it seemed to Andrew to be an apt term. The peddlers called on the agency account people servicing the client, as well as the agency media planners to tell their stories and present their numbers. Historically this segment of the advertising business played a lot of golf, slapped a lot of backs and left folders filled with computer printouts of numbers wherever they went.

Lunch loomed large in the lives of old-timers. Unfortunately, their business had changed dramatically in recent years. One reason was that decisions about what media to choose revolved more around numbers and less around personal selling, entertainment and the like. Another reason was that some of their customers, the media planners, were different.

The new breed of planners was much younger, in their 20's. They were predominantly females, who were perpetually perky, efficient, and so computerized they had numbers on top of numbers.

It was tough to win them over with just lunch. This new species didn't even eat lunch. They worked out, brown-bagged it or did something else at lunchtime.

Andrew wondered how these sales reps who called on media planners could hack it. You made a jillion calls, but you hardly ever got a yes or no to your proposal. In essence, you never knew when you made a sale. Someone at the advertising agency presented your case to the client, days or even weeks later. The yes or no might come weeks after that. No wonder some of the peddlers were still doing the gin and tonic lunches waiting for answers, when they weren't calling on the Andrews of the world.

It was too late to cancel lunch. But maybe he could pick up some intelligence on the ENNU situation. God knows he needed to find out something about what Simon Slater was up to.

NEW YORK, 12:45 P.M.

Norman had spent the morning getting ready for the Associated Foods visit the next week. Every new business opportunity was do or die. Norman's belief was that an agency was either on the way up, winning business, or on the way down, losing it. If you lost a few accounts you could go into a downward spiral, a situation that was extremely difficult to reverse. First, the press got on you, suggesting the agency wasn't what it used to be. Then other competitive agencies in town started calling your clients. Then your people started wondering if they were working at the right place. If you didn't stop the slide, you could go all the way into the tank.

It was hard to keep his mind on the new business encounter now that the Board meeting was happening so quickly. He wondered how he would be able to get to Bunker and Arness before the meeting, and to touch base with Andrew again.

Taking a break from his Associated Foods meetings, he placed calls to Bunker and Arness. He managed to reach Bunker's secretary who promised to have the Chicagoan call back as soon as he was able. All Norman was able to accomplish with Arness was to connect with his voice mail.

Norman called his secretary to arrange to eat in. He had to be in his office to take his two critical calls. His future was calling.

CHICAGO, 12:45 P.M.

Hanging up the phone after his conversation with Norman, Bunker frowned and began to idly rearrange his golf ball collection. He suddenly found himself squarely in the middle of the WJR situation. What a pain in the ass. Of course, he felt badly about Will's passing, he was worried about Emily, and he was deeply concerned about the WJR financial problem. But, now he also felt thrust into the role of kingmaker.

Norman wanted his vote.

Surely Eric wanted his support.

Sir George not only wanted his support, he wanted Sandy to lead the charge that would push through the sale of WJR to the Englishman. None of this was what Bunker had in mind when he agreed to become a director of WJR. He had simply wanted to keep an eye on the bank's money. And the 25k was a nice addition to his personal cash flow.

Sandy Bunker had a reputation of being one of the best commercial lenders in town. While his background was not remarkable in any way, everything in his formative years seemed to point him in the direction of his banking career.

A Chicago area native, Sandy was a popular youngster growing up His gregarious nature and willingness to pitch in on various activities led to becoming a class officer in both his sophomore and senior years. Medium in size and not really athletic in build, he was considered good looking, maybe "cute," but not handsome, by the opposite sex and someone you like hanging around with, by the guys. All in all, Bunker was considered a "likely to succeed" candidate. A good, but not exceptional student, he had a special knack for economics, which he studied at the University of Illinois at Champaign. In college, Bunker attracted a gaggle of nicknames. Besides Sandy, he was called Bonkers, Binky, Bunky and for a while, even Eddy. Sandy stuck with him throughout his adult years.

Meeting his wife at a fraternity beer party, Sandy married immediately after graduation, and returned to the Chicago area where he interviewed for a variety of positions in the financial services area. As he joined the Mercantile Bank training program, he also enrolled in the University of Chicago's Downtown MBA program. Because he intended to remain in Chicago, he felt that the Illinois and Chicago MBA connection were important. Bunker had learned early on about the importance of contacts. It was particularly germane to success in the Chicago banking business.

Working his way up through the ranks of the Mercantile Bank, Bunker became a member of the right clubs, established a wide circle of relationships, and eventually he became one of the business leaders in Chicago. Now 55, he had a big house on the lake in Lake Forest, the charity-involved wife, three photogenic, reasonably well-adjusted children, and the decorator-appointed second home in a golf course community on Florida's East coast. Everything was going his way. Until the WJR gaff, anyway.

Bunker reflected upon his telephone conversation with Norman, who obviously was not shy about advancing his candidacy. He was not surprised at the New Yorker's pushiness in going for the brass ring. Bunker knew you couldn't be a shrinking violet and be good at new business. He had to admit, though, that Norman's concept of "people who run the business should run the business" was compelling. As a line officer himself, dealing directly with customers and having an effect on the bank's success, Sandy Bunker admired those people who made businesses run.

Norman had been confident—even firm—about having the L.A. lady behind him, but he also admitted that Andrew Miller might not be totally committed to the New Yorker. There was no mention of Hanson.

The discussion with Norman did not cause the banker to reach a decision on the CEO matter. Maybe he should have a conversation with Andrew Miller. Certainly, he also needed to talk to Hanson. And Arness, wherever he was. Realizing that he was a swing vote— maybe *the* swing vote–however, seemed to put a lot of weight squarely on his shoulders. Maybe that was appropriate, he thought, because of the Bank's position with WJR.

So there was no getting around it. He had to make a decision, *the* decision.

It was a dilemma.

To broaden his options, he put in a call to London. Sir George would be officially invited to the WJR Sunday board meeting.

CHICAGO, 2:00 P.M.

Having returned from lunch with Kimberly, Andrew returned to the problem at hand—how to get to Simon Slater at ENNU. Unfortunately, the space rep had been no help at all.

After Simon's letter to WJR about reviewing the advertising, Andrew had answered with a letter to Simon introducing himself, then followed up with a phone call. The ENNU president had not returned his call, but his secretary did phone Andrew to advise him that the ENNU executive was too busy to get back to him now, and would contact him when the dust settled. When you're running an advertising agency, you learn to be paranoid, and Andrew immediately thought the worst. How could someone in charge of a heavily advertised brand be "too busy" to talk to the head of his ad agency?

Sitting on his sofa, feet up on the coffee table, Andrew scribbled on a pad of paper.

He had just jotted down the headline of a new ad for ENNU,

"WE'VE GOT NIKE ON THE RUN."

Pretty good, he thought. It could be the next ad in the "Watch Out Nike" campaign.

Andrew believed that WJR could keep their powerful ENNU campaign going if he could just get to Simon.

He dialed Laura Forbes.

"Laura, can you come in? I want to talk about ENNU."

"I'm there," she answered.

Within a minute, Laura Forbes, Senior VP of client service, walked into Andrew's office without knocking. As his senior lieutenant in Chicago, she had full access to the boss. Laura carried a plain folder holding some papers.

"How's it going?" she asked with a smile.

"It's going shitty, that's how it's going. How can you smile at a time like this?" A little snippy for the normally even-tempered leader.

"Hey, you're the one who's hammered at me all these years about keeping a game face, no matter what's going on."

Andrew knew she was right and managed a wry smile.

Now buoyed by Laura's demeanor, Andrew motioned her to sit down.

"We've got to get to Simon somehow. He's not answering my calls. I figure you've already started to find out about him...where he went to school, where he lives, does he play golf, where he's worked. You know, the whole dossier."

"I started the search a week ago," answered Laura. "We've been on the Internet, checked all the business directories, and gone through the California stuff where he worked for awhile, plus some other sources."

Andrew nodded approvingly at her competency. "Great. What do you have?"

"It seems you two have a lot in common. Slater's a good consumer marketer. Supposed to be a good guy. A Midwesterner went to Grinnell College. Navy officer. Plays golf."

"Do you know where and how he got his Navy commission?" asked Andrew. "Maybe there's a connection."

"I'll find out and put it in the report."

"Way to go," said Andrew.

"I've been thinking about what to talk about when we do get to him," offered Laura, as she got up and moved about the office.

"Before you get started, take a look at this," interrupted Andrew, shoving the ad headline he penned across the desk toward her.

"Not bad...but it's too close to the current campaign," said Laura. One of the things Andrew liked about Laura was that she told him the truth. It was hard to get the truth out of most of the people who worked for you.

Laura continued, "Our campaign is working like crazy, but new management people always want a new campaign, their own campaign. You and I know that it's really stupid to change something that's working, so let's keep the same position, 'Watch Out Nike', but take the campaign to a different level."

"Okay," agreed Andrew.

"Look, everyone in the business has been doing this lifestyle shit or the 'my endorser is better than your endorser' stuff. Every shoe manufacturer is trying to either get inside your mind or inside your jock. I mean we're just talking about shoes here to work out, run, play basketball, whatever. It's not like you need a certain brand of shoes to win World War III."

"I'm with you so far," said Andrew intrigued.

"So, everyone is telling you that you can emulate one superstar or another, or is talking about changing your life with their shoes," she continued, "But there's one thing no one is doing."

"What's that," asked Andrew, pretty sure he knew where she was going with this thinking.

"No one's talking about why their shoe is better than all the other guys. And with a pair running (no pun intended) a hundred bucks or more, it's time to do the kind of advertising that justifies the price. The market has matured, now it should be 'my shoes are better than your shoes' not 'my jock is better than your jock'.

"Our stuff is saying we're better than the other guys."

"Right, but we really aren't telling the market why."

"I think you're onto it," said Andrew grinning and getting excited.

"Here's my lead ad," said Laura, opening her folder and pulling out some papers,

"TWENTY-ONE WAYS WE COULD HAVE SKIMPED
ON YOUR ENNU. BUT DIDN'T."

Long copy, all the facts, imported rubber from Brazil, all the tech superiority. Here's my other core ad,

"WHAT NIKE DOESN'T WANT YOU TO KNOW."

"Jesus, this is good," exclaimed Andrew. "Did you write these yourself?"

"Well, I had a couple of drinks with the creatives after work and we tossed some stuff around. And now they think it's their idea," she said coyly.

"So we're keeping the same "WATCH OUT" position...we're not saying that what we're doing wasn't working, and we're taking a fresh look at the category, "said Andrew. I like it a lot. Let's get some people to turn this into something we can show."

"Thanks. I'm going to get this moving," said Laura heading for the door.

Andrew felt a sense of accomplishment in her competence. Will had always told him, "We can't promote you until you have a successor." He had begun to groom Laura for his job during the last 18 months. She was smart, tough and knew how to get superior work out of others.

Andrew had his successor. The only problem was that his champion had passed on to that big agency in the sky.

MAUNA LANI, HAWAII, 10:00 A.M.

Waggling his brand new oversize metal driver, Arness squinted into the sun down the third fairway. His first two drives had been god-awful; he couldn't keep the ball on the fairway. Pretty dumb he thought. Buying a new and unfamiliar weapon to take to a strange, unfamiliar golf course. This drive needed to be good. There was water to the right and what looked like serious jungle to the left.

After a leisurely breakfast outside on the hotel terrace, Leon and Diana had driven to a golf course down the coast with a couple from the U.K. they had met in the cocktail lounge the night before. They were a charming, fun loving twosome to spend some time with and both were accomplished golfers. Playing with them today was much better than being paired with total strangers.

Arness had thought about calling his office, but remembered that his secretary was off today; one of several days off he had encouraged her to take. There was a nagging feeling that something was left undone, but he couldn't put his finger on it. The hell with it, let 'em try and find me he thought, as he smacked a high lazy hook away from the water, but drifting dangerously close to the jungle.

NEW YORK, 4:00 P.M.

Norman was relieved to be able to discuss his point of view with Sandy Bunker, who had called him back relatively quickly. While

105

noncommittal, the outside director did seem receptive to the idea about the people who were running the business.

Reaching Arness was something else. All he got in calling Leon's office was his answering machine. Obviously, his secretary was also not available. Norman tried to figure out what was going on. Was he just out of the office but might return later? Was he out of town? If so, maybe he was gone for several days.

Norman's analytical mind kicked in. He had only a few hours today to locate Arness. If he weren't out of town, he would probably call back. He would wait a short time, but after that Norman couldn't take the chance. He would have to assume that Leon was on the road somewhere. How to find him?

Not having a home phone number, Norman went onto the Internet phone search. He was in luck. Dialing Leon's home number, Norman was elated to hear a live voice on the other end of the line. It was the housekeeper. He explained who he was. Although the skittish housekeeper wouldn't reveal Arness' whereabouts, Norman convinced her to promise to get a message off quickly.

After Norman hung up she did indeed call the Big Island with a message. "Norman Steinberg needs to talk to you before board meeting. Very important. Please call his office. Leave message where you can be reached."

LOS ANGELES, 2:15 P.M.

Marcy leaned against the black painted wall and surveyed the activity in the warehouse-like building. Three or four people at the center of things were moving floodlights on stands. Another two dozen or so other people appeared to be simply standing around with their hands in their pockets. Some of them were stuffing themselves from a long table of food. By and large it was a scruffy group in t-shirts, jeans, leather vests and the like. To any outsider, it would appear there was at least three times the number of people than were needed to do whatever it was they were doing.

It was a television shoot.

Today, Marcy's job was to keep the client off the director's back so he could do his job. Some clients were always under foot, wanting to contribute, to rewrite, to change. Some clients were simply "star fuckers" who loved to hang around with celebrity presenters. Actually, they were the easiest to control. They were busy being star struck so you didn't have to worry about them changing everything and getting in the director's way.

She deftly steered today's client away from the scene being shot and accompanied him to check out the product to be on camera in the next scene.

A production assistant interrupted, "Phone call, Ms. Gallipo. Says it's important."

Andrew had dialed Marcy at WJR/LA. Ethel took the call. "If it's important, I can get to her...she's on a shoot."

"It's important."

"Okay. Give me a minute, I'll transfer you," answered Ethel.

"This is Marcy."

"Hey, what's going on?" asked Andrew.

"Wild. But it must be the same for you," she answered guardedly.

"I understand you're busy on a shoot, so I'll get to the point. I talked to Norman about what he wants."

"Oh. Me, too. What do you think?" asked Marcy.

"I'm not sure. What's your take?" Andrew wanted to know where Marcy stood.

"I think Norman's right. Look, the three of us have to stick together," pressed Marcy.

"So you think Norman is the one to run the show?"

"Well look, I don't want to hurt your feelings, but he's got a well thought out plan. I think it works for the whole company. Besides New York is the biggest office. I know we don't want that dumb viking in charge. He doesn't have a plan and he doesn't have a clue. Do you really think he knows what makes this business tick?"

"Well, he's been around for awhile," said Andrew, somewhat defensively.

"Being around and being capable are two different things," she said. "You remember the old Norwegian joke?" she said, suddenly softening.

"Which one?"

"After God made Norway, he looked down on the country and said, 'Listen, act dumb until I get back'."

Andrew couldn't help but chuckle. "That's pretty good. Well, at least I'm going to hear him out. I think I owe him that."

"For hanging around?"

"Yep, for hanging around. Hey, thanks for taking the call. See you before the board meeting. Gotta go. I have to do something I can't put off."

Marcy hung up, thinking she should call Norman about the conversation. She decided not to, having no idea which way Andrew was leaning. Could he torpedo Norman's plan in league with the outside directors? It was possible.

CHICAGO, 4:20 P.M.

As he replaced the phone, Andrew had his answer about Marcy. She was solidly in Norman's camp.

Perhaps it was worthwhile to meet with Norman before the board meeting to find out what assurances he could extract from the New Yorker.

He asked his secretary, June, to get in touch with Norman to arrange a meeting before the Saturday evening dinner with Eric and Sadie Hanson. Also to get dinner reservations at LaScala—four at seven. This would be interesting and probably very revealing...to meet with the two contenders the night before they stepped into the ring.

Andrew prepared himself for an unpleasant task. Firing Billy Shipley. Everyone liked Billy; agency people, client people, media people. Andrew liked Billy, too. But he wasn't cutting it at WJR. Billy had to go.

To make matters worse, it was Friday. All the personnel experts said don't fire someone on the last workday of a week because the person will have all weekend to brood about it. That was too much time for a spouse, significant other or someone else to pump up the victim with, "You march in there Monday and tell them they can't do that to you!"

Andrew had decided he couldn't wait any longer to move on Billy. By now the rest of the agency, particularly the young Turks were probably wondering, "Hey, this guy is a bunky. What's the matter with management? Don't they know he doesn't have the goods? Why don't they sack him? Am I working at the right place?"

Andrew had terminated people more times than he wished to remember, but that did not make this situation any easier. He believed that one of the qualities that made him a good manager was that he was willing to deliver the bad news to employees. The thing to worry about was that you didn't want to find yourself liking it.

Andrew cleared his throat and dialed Billy.

CHICAGO, 5:20 P.M.

Sandy and Eric clinked glasses and dispensed with the small talk about the 4A's meeting, Eric's flight, and the fierce traffic into town on a Friday afternoon. The setting was the Guild Club, one of the top two or three downtown clubs in Chicago. The Windy City has always been a clubby town. Most of the business executives of the city preferred private settings as places to do business. The Guild Club was a conclave of advertising people, journalists, business executives and political figures.

The two men were seated at Eric's favorite table overlooking Michigan Avenue. They were surrounded by the blonde wood paneled walls—paneled about halfway up the wall as if it were wainscoting. The upper half of the walls was covered by red-flocked wallpaper. The chairs were all red, green and gold prints, as was the carpet. It was funky and unique, and most of the members would have strongly resisted any attempt to change the decor.

"Well, Eric. What's going on? I'm wondering why you're jamming through this board meeting," said Sandy. "What's the hurry?"

Eric took a deep breath and began. "That's a good question. One of the points I wanted to stress with you was that we need to solve the succession problem quickly," answered Eric. "The longer the uncertainty of who's in charge goes on, the worse it is for WJR. In our business, if your competitors smell blood, they come in for the kill. They're like piranhas. I don't believe we should wait two weeks to settle succession. Besides, in this case a meeting is convenient. Everyone will be in for Will's services. Anyway, in my mind, the choice is relatively simple. There's really no need to stretch this out. I am the senior officer of the company. I've been close to Will all along," he added.

"As the senior officer of WJR, maybe it would be helpful if you outline the possible choices for me," suggested Sandy, leaning forward and raising his eyebrows slightly. As perverse as it seemed, he was beginning to enjoy this.

Eric coughed nervously. "Well, of course on paper you could make a case that there are several choices," he replied. "It's possible that a general manager could move up into the big job. But it's one thing to run an operational unit, and it's another thing to oversee the operations of an entire business."

"I would agree with that in principle," acknowledged Bunker.

"Let me get to the point," said Eric. "I think that almost everyone inside and outside of the company would expect the former number two person to move up," he said sallying forth again. "I have the experience, the knowledge, and..."

"What's expected is not always what's right," interrupted Bunker. "We can't let ourselves be influenced by what outsiders expect."

Eric pressed on. "You need to understand that I'm really Will's hand-picked successor. We talked about this frequently."

"How can I be sure about that?" asked Bunker, his eyes narrowing.

"You'll just have to take my word for it, Sandy," said Eric, who forced a smile that he hoped would appear friendly.

Both men were becoming uncomfortable with the direction of the conversation. Bunker decided to back off a bit. Perhaps Eric had indeed been Will's choice as next in line. He really didn't know that he wasn't.

"What about the support of the GM's?" asked Bunker. "If you were to get my vote, who else is behind you?"

"I'm pretty sure Andrew will support me," replied Eric, buoyed by the question. "I really don't know about the others." He hoped, desperately, that the question of the vote of Leon Arness did not surface in this conversation.

It didn't.

"What do you know about the agency's line of credit?" queried Bunker, changing the conversation abruptly.

Eric was caught off guard.

"I'm really not, uhh, current on that," he stammered. What the hell was *this* all about?

Bunker debated with himself whether to press on. He did.

"You mean you are not aware of the financial situation of your agency?" asked Bunker, surprised, but also distressed that "Mr. Number Two" didn't have a clue about the financial crisis.

"Well, while we talked about operations in the monthly meetings, Will kept the balance sheet part of the business pretty much to himself," replied Eric.

Bunker decided the financial situation had to be brought out into the open with the managers, and be a factor in the succession process.

"Eric, I have to tell you that your company is close to being maxed out on your line of credit. Your equity situation is poor, and you have a serious, maybe critical, cash flow problem."

Eric felt a panic grip him. Shit. Not only was his solicitation of Bunker's support not going well, now he had to contend with this financial problem as well.

"Adding new business is always the answer to revenue and ultimately cash flow problems," said Eric, trying to stay calm. "It's an income business."

"Then what about Norman as CEO?" asked Bunker, abruptly switching gears again. "Isn't he your new business whiz?"

Not ready for this question, Eric appeared flustered. Another forced smile. He paused to collect his thoughts. "Well, he's a great new business guy, probably a good ad guy, too. But, he's a New Yorker, and this is a Chicago company. We're talking oil and water."

"As you said, though, new business is the best answer to cash flow problems and that's Norman's skill," countered Sandy.

Eric did not answer. He was out of smiles.

Sandy was pleased with his ability to maintain control of the conversation, but he wondered that this was too easy. Could this guy run a big time ad agency?

"What about Andrew?" asked Bunker, shifting the focus on the conversation again. "I haven't spent much time with him, but he always seemed to have a wide range of leadership skills."

"Andrew is a very good man," replied Eric. "He has no major flaws. Someday he'll be a great CEO. Perhaps after I move on out of the company. But, he simply isn't ready now."

"Not enough time in grade?" asked Bunker.

"Exactly."

"So, by process of elimination, you feel you're the obvious choice?"

"I'd rather put it in a more positive light."

"This has been an interesting discussion," said Bunker, glancing at his watch. "I've got to get to a dinner date."

"Sandy, I want you to know that your support is critical. With your guidance I'm sure we'll bring the cash flow situation into a proper balance."

"It may take more than my guidance," replied Bunker. "I'm going to think this through before I give you an answer. If you don't mind, I have to run."

He did not have to run, but it was obvious that this conversation had nowhere to go. The meeting was over.

"Go ahead, Sandy. I'll take care of this."

Bunker rose from his chair, shook hands with Eric and headed for the doorway.

Left alone and thoroughly deflated, Eric signed the Guild Club ticket and entered his club number. Watching Bunker wind his way past the tables toward the front door, he reflected on what had transpired. This encounter had not gone well at all. At this point, he had no idea whether or not he had Bunker's vote. He couldn't even keep him on a track—he kept changing the subject. The man was infuriating.

As Bunker headed for the street where he would be met by the Merc limo, he reflected on the meeting. His take was that Eric had some limitations but might be able to do the job. Norman also had limitations, but in Bunker's mind, he appeared to have some leadership qualities. Surrounding all the intrigue was the British factor.

Sandy knew he had the deciding vote. It was still a dilemma.

#

Still frustrated by his meeting with Bunker, Eric hailed a cab and headed North on Lake Shore Drive toward his Gold Coast apartment. The traffic was bumper to bumper, moving more slowly than usual. Not only was he in the midst of the normal Friday evening traffic, there was a rare Friday night baseball game at Wrigley Field, as well. Resolving to calm down, he forced himself to use the time to review his options again. There was no way to determine what Bunker would do. Would further pursuit of him bear fruit? Hard to tell. Indeed, Bunker may already be in his camp, but simply unwilling to commit himself publicly at this time.

It was now imperative to get Andrew on board to support him. At least he would have the opportunity at dinner tomorrow to win him over. Was Andrew agreeing to have dinner with spouses a signal that the Chicago manager felt positively about Eric? Would this be a one-big-happy-family dinner? Or was Andrew attending reluctantly and planning to use Sally as a protective shield to avoid a commitment? Shaking his head glumly, Eric decided there was no way to know until they actually met and spent some time together.

What if Andrew rebuffed him? What then? A solution—at least a reaction—came to him: If he failed to win Andrew and then things were going badly for him in the board meeting, he would scuttle the entire meeting. Since he was the self-appointed presiding director, and no one had yet challenged his assumption of that post, he would simply table the election, and perhaps even stalk out of the room, leaving the other four wondering what to do next. Believing that this was a last-ditch option, Eric decided to tuck it into the back of his mind, to be retrieved on Sunday.

It was a negative thought, however, and the wrong frame of mind in which to pursue the next phase of "Operation UFFDA."

That was the winning of Andrew. Could he pull it off?

HAWAII, 1:30 P.M.

Picking up his key at the front desk, Leon was handed a message, which he stuffed in his golf shorts on the way to the bar to meet Diana and the British couple. That would teach him to check.

As the foursome settled in at the bar overlooking the pool, he peeled open the message. It was from Norman. Leon was puzzled.

Why would it be important that Norman talk to him before the next board meeting. That wasn't for another couple of weeks anyway. Why reach him here in Hawaii? Unusual, thought Leon. Well, plenty of time to get back to him next week.

Anyway, Norman wasn't his client. Will was.

NEW YORK, 6:45 P.M.

Still at the office, Norman despaired at reaching Arness. Either Leon's housekeeper didn't do what she said she was going to do, or Arness simply didn't get the message. Or perhaps he got the message but ignored it. Reaching into his pocket Norman pulled out the piece of paper and unfolded "The Norman Conquest."

He had his own and Marcy's vote. Not being able to reach Arness before the board meeting meant that he somehow had to sell him just before or during the meeting, and hope that Bunker went along with him. Norman's mind raced ahead to the meeting. What would Eric say to advance his own candidacy? He'd spent the last few years caddying for Will. Good thing Eric didn't know about the bank mess.

What would be the best way to present his own case? The answer was clear. He smiled. The best way to sell his candidacy to the two outside directors was to document the success, the power and the promise of the New York office of WJR. The numbers were the numbers. Perhaps a report in the form of a deck would be more appropriate than a hard sell presentation. Lots of numbers, lots of support.

He began to type on his computer, updating the current year's forecast, which so far was looking good. The basic forecast showed that New York would reach $220 million in billings of the total company's $480. Norman then hyped the numbers by listing all the potential new business billings that New York was currently pitching. The total was $90 million, including the $50 million of Associated Foods. This was looking good, thought Norman. With any luck at all, New York will add up to more than half of WJR. Just getting the Associated account would do it. He would make the point that WJR/New York was the favorite for this new business win. So it wasn't quite true. Who could prove otherwise? He was the best man to lead the company. A lot of jobs depended upon him. If he had to fudge the nums to get the job, ultimately it was good for the company.

Deciding to forego dinner, Norman called his dinner partner and begged off because of the board meeting. It was the truth. He had a report to prepare. He returned to his computer and his report. Should he include the revenue from the bank? The account that was poised to walk out the door? Why not. Technically, it was still an account.

NORTHFIELD, ILLINOIS, 6:30 P.M.

As Bunker's car wound its way North along the expressway, he decided to try reaching Arness again. Even though the two men were not really friends, he now considered Leon an ally. Calling from the car, he tried Leon's home number and reached the housekeeper just as Norman had. Again she refused to reveal the whereabouts of her master, but of course, would get this important message "To call Mr. Bunker" to him.

Traveling homeward, Sandy Bunker leaned back and nestled into the black leather back seat of the Sedan Deville. The car with driver was his favorite perk. In his mind, it was also one of the most justifiable. The ride to and from work gave him an opportunity to get things done without fear of being interrupted. Sandy was able to dispose of most of his lower priority reading during the trip home, which took an hour to an hour and a half, depending upon the traffic.

Today Sandy had been through a very active day and tonight was a night out. He set the papers aside figuring he could get to them over the weekend. In fact, almost everything could wait until he got

through this WJR mess. He still couldn't believe he had gotten himself into this situation. He resolved to figure a way out tomorrow
morning.

Then he nodded off.

#

Two miles eastward, Andrew sat in his living room dressed for
the evening after a refreshing shower. He and Sally were scheduled
to be at a neighborhood cocktail party 20 minutes ago. To call this
another tough day at the office was an understatement. The culmina-
tion of the day, his termination of Billy, was even more painful and
drawn out than he had imagined.

Billy was shocked at the company's action. Even though he
agreed with Andrew that perhaps there had been some gaps in his
performance, in his mind the firing was "out of the blue." First he
had broken into tears and told Andrew about some money problems.
Then he became angry and accused the general manager of not giving him a real chance to succeed. Finally, he pleaded with Andrew
for another chance, an opportunity to improve his performance while
he got back on his feet financially. Andrew wouldn't be sorry.

Having rehearsed carefully the company's stance and his own ver-
biage, Andrew stuck to his guns. While he felt badly personally, he
told Billy his on-the-job performance was substandard. It was unfor-
tunate about Billy's financial situation but surely he understood that
the company could not make personnel decisions based on individual
employee financial situations. Obviously, that wouldn't be fair to the
other employees.

Andrew decided to end the conversation by re-stating the termination terms. Over the years he had learned you had to tell everything twice to the person you were firing. The first time, he or she
were usually so shocked, the terms didn't sink in. Andrew had re-
stated everything to Billy and then offered outplacement services to
him. Of course the company would pay for the services.

Billy glared at Andrew. "So that's it?"

"I'm afraid so, Billy."

"This isn't fair." He gripped the arms of the chair tightly with both hands.

Billy paused a moment and made some notes on the yellow pad of paper he had brought to the meeting. Then he rose, turned on his heel and stalked out of Andrew's office, slamming the door.

"I'll be back. With a lawyer," he shouted through the door.

LOS ANGELES, 8:30 P.M.

Having finished up her travel arrangements for Saturday, Marcy began dressing for her evening engagement. She was scheduled to arrive in Chicago late tomorrow afternoon in time for dinner with Norman. Plenty of time to pack tomorrow morning.

This had been a day of doing a lot of things she didn't want to do. She didn't want to interview Clete (although she was glad she did), didn't want to go on the shoot, and didn't want to have dinner with Raul. Oh well, it was the price of being the big cahuna. Cahuness?

The dinner with Raul was not at all what she expected. Being ready for anything—a knock-down-drag-out business discussion, an attack on WJR/LA, or a sexual advance, Marcy was surprised that Raul spent the entire evening talking about the wife who didn't understand him. It became evident that her job for the evening was to listen. She relaxed and played the role, alternating between shaking her head with understanding and saying "umm" in sympathy.

She decided to wait until dessert to pre-sell the two campaigns to be presented the next week. Unfortunately, Raul decided to leave without dessert. He had to get home. She had missed her chance.

Shit. He was as unpredictable as they come.

HAWAII, 9:30 P.M.

The dinner overlooking the pounding surf had been a pleasant one. The wind had come up, although the temperature was still mild. Leon and Diana, as well as their new British golfing companions, all had too many Pina Coladas before dinner, and too much Chardonnay during. Treading a little unsteadily past the front desk, Leon checked once more for messages. Shit. Another one. Entering the elevator, Arness opened the envelope and read Bunker's message.

> "Important we talk before board meeting Sunday. Please call me at home. 847-561-5858."

Sunday? What board meeting, wondered Leon? What the hell's going on here? He glanced at his watch as the elevator doors opened. Let's see...it was 2:30 a.m. in Chicago. He'd have to call tomorrow. Serves him right. For Christ sakes, I'm on vacation.

Saturday

With everything that was going on with WJR and ENNU, Andrew felt somewhat guilty going to the golf course. He overcame the feeling by deciding he needed a mental break from it all.

Walking into the red brick colonial clubhouse onto the lavish green carpet framed by wildly flowered wallpaper of pink, green and yellow, Andrew couldn't help but smile. Most of the members hated the old wallpaper with a passion. Andrew loved it because it was colorful and elegant in a funky way, and why not have this kind of decor in your club, because your wife would never let it in the front door of your home.

He turned into the entrance of the dark walnut-paneled men's locker room and headed down the hallway, which displayed portraits of past presidents dating back to 1895.

It was Andrew's love of golf that caused him to join the club at 36, but it turned out to be a great help in his business life. In Chicago, golf and business mixed well. During the course of the golf season, Andrew met and played with many prospective clients. Spending time on the golf course also helped solidify relationships with existing clients, too. More than once it was at the bar after a round of golf with a client when he had learned that the account was in trouble...people loosened up and would tell you things in that setting that they just didn't reveal in their offices.

While playing golf was a joy, some of the country club baggage that came with it amused and sometimes amazed him. For a place and a setting where things apparently were going so well, there was always a small group of vocal complainers. Some people complained about the condition of the course, some complained about the food, some about the service. And some people simply complained about everything (their role in life), including the other complainers. Andrew tried to avoid all the conversations about sacking the manager, replacing the pro, revising the dress code, changing the beer on draft, or changing anything else that hadn't been changed in the last five years.

The thing he loved about golf is that it was unlike any other sport in the way participants obeyed the rules. In football you tried to fake a catch even though you actually trapped the ball. In basketball, you tried to convince the ref you took a "charge" even though you actually blocked the offensive player. Players tried to get away with penalties in hockey, baseball catchers attempted to make balls look like strikes by moving their gloves after catching the ball. Anything to win.

Golf was different. If your drive was out of bounds by inches, you were expected to call it on yourself. If you hit someone else's ball, you called a two-stroke penalty on yourself. If you somehow touched the sand when addressing the ball in a bunker, you called it. It wasn't like most other sports. Instead of doing anything to win, you tried to do the right thing–and still hoped you'd win. Andrew liked that.

He usually just showed up on a Saturday morning to get a game. You didn't need tee times, unlike some of the other clubs. Besides, he liked to play with new people. Who knows, you might meet a new business prospect. Today, Ralph, the head locker room attendant set him up with a game.

For a few hours anyway, he could forget about business, his future and everything else.

CHICAGO, 9:00 A.M.

Dressed in khakis, sneakers and yesterday's button down blue shirt, Eric sat at his desk on WJR's executive floor. Normally on a May Saturday morning, he might be strolling along the lake near the harbor watching some of Chicago's sailors put their boats in the water for the season. He frequently wondered whether he should get a boat and learn to sail. He always dismissed the thought.

Today, Eric was leafing rapidly through the by-laws of W.J. Raffensberger, Inc., a Delaware Corporation. He found the section he was looking for.

There it was in black and white. It was the Board's responsibility to fill Will's slot. The by-laws not only allowed Eric to push for this board meeting, they *required* the directors to act.

Eric thumbed back through the by-law pages looking for the other section of importance. As he found it and started reading, he began to smile.

SECTION 7. SPECIAL MEETINGS OF THE BOARD
MAY BE CALLED BY THE CHIEF EXECUTIVE OF-
FICER OR PRESIDENT ON TWO DAYS NOTICE TO
EACH DIRECTOR, EITHER PERSONALLY OR BY
MAIL OR BY TELEGRAM; SPECIAL MEETINGS
MAY BE CALLED BY THE SECRETARY IN A LIKE
MANNER OR ON LIKE NOTICE ON THE WRITTEN
REQUEST OF TWO DIRECTORS.

Eric laughed out loud, delighted with himself and his luck. "MAY BE CALLED BY THE SECRETARY IN A LIKE MANNER." As the secretary of WJR, he was well within his rights to call the special board meeting...on his own written request. That must have been in there back in the old days when Emily was the secretary and a director to enable Emily to act if something happened to Will, he thought. These had to be the original by-laws—nobody sent telegrams anymore.

Eric packed up the brown leather-clad by-laws book and stuffed it into his briefcase with some of his stacked up mail. He now had the ammunition he needed for Sunday if challenged on his authority to call a meeting and pursue the election. But what if he wasn't the only one who had a copy of the by-laws? Something to think about.

ERIE PENNSYLVANIA, 10:30 A.M.

At 30,000 feet, Norman relaxed in first class. He was wondering how Eric ever got as far as he did. Probably because he was the classic high school hero, the football star, class president-type. Not real bright, but he looked the part. Some others like Eric also made it to the top in advertising.

In Norman's opinion, most of the ad biggies he knew were the other type, the "outies". These were people on the outside who never got elected to anything in high school and were either too fat or too ugly or too ethnic as kids. Some of them wore thick glasses and led the league in acne. A lot of the "outies" were driven to overcome their early shortcomings and social problems, and ended up succeeding in later life.

Besides, advertising people weren't identified early in life, anyway. Nobody says, "Boy, he'll make a good advertising man." Maybe a great engineer. Or a minister. Or a doctor. Or lawyer. But not an advertising man.

Norman was determined that the Eric football hero type was not going to run WJR. It was going to be Norman, the "outie." The one who really knew the business, who lived in the business, who worked in the business, who grew the business.

LAKE FOREST, 11:30 A.M.

The waves pounded the shore displacing some of the dark brown coarse sand and pebbles along the narrow beach. Erosion was a continuing problem along Lake Michigan's Southwest shore. Alone in a metal beach chair, clad in Levis and a "River Club" sweat shirt, Sandy put down his book, an historical novel. He was on the beach below his house, which rested 60 feet above him on the bluffs that ringed Lake Michigan in this area. In spite of the simple pastoral setting—sand, lake and sky—today it was difficult for him to relax and read, one of his favorite Saturday morning pastimes. It was time to deal with the WJR situation.

He thought back to his conversation with Emily and his explanation of the WJR buy/sell agreement. The advertising agency was approaching a negative net worth situation. As with many privately held advertising agencies, the net worth was quite low compared to the company's revenues because the objective of these firms was not to build equity, but to pay money out to the owners in good years. Obviously, the WJR current value would be way down because of last year's bankrupt client and this year's low or negative earnings. Should he call Emily to alert her? He immediately dismissed the thought; not now, she had enough to worry about.

124

The good news for the young Turks at WJR was that they could buy the company from Emily on the cheap. If they could get financing. Bunker heaved a large sigh as he realized whom they would come to for financing. Not a sure thing, he thought. I might have to send them packing and have the bank take its lumps. The buy/sell agreement did allow a year to make the buy, however.

Pushing that distasteful thought of financing the buyout from his mind, he wondered what Emily's situation was. He knew that Will had a very large split dollar life insurance policy on himself. Company paid, of course. Emily would get 50% of the proceeds and 50% would go to the company, presumably to somewhat offset the loss of the CEO to the company. Bunker had forgotten about the insurance payout to the company; it would provide some much needed cash flow, and also provide some of the funds to buy Emily's stock.

Emily would probably be okay, he thought. He knew that over the years Will had taken out large amounts from the profits of WJR. That was why equity had remained at a low level. The visible evidence of Will's distribution of the WJR wealth was the house in Vail and the big spread in Tucson. Yes, Emily would be all right.

He picked up his book and resolved to relax for a while.

WINNETKA, 12:15 P.M.

In spite of all the distractions of the week and a slight hangover, today Andrew had a good round of golf going. A fourteen handicap, he had fashioned a very spiffy 40 on the front nine and was only two over par on the back nine, as he approached the 16th hole. He had a legitimate chance to break 80, something he had done less than 10 times in his life.

His drive on the 16th hole was striped down the middle and his second shot was a perfect three iron, also laced down the center of the fairway on the 490-yard par five. He had chosen an iron to play it safe so that the second shot would not carry into the lake that fronted the smallish, mounded sixteenth green. Pulling his pitching wedge out of the bag, he was determined to hit it crisply toward the center of the green. It was as good a swing as he made all day, but a blustery left to right breeze gripped the ball and carried it to the right edge of the green, where it hit at the top of the mound, remained there for an agonizing period of time and then slowly trickled down the slope, where it gained speed and finally plopped softly into the lake. He couldn't believe it. Another six inches, maybe only three inches higher and the shot would have rolled onto the green in ideal position for his par, perhaps even a birdie. All because of an unforeseen gust of wind.

Crestfallen, Andrew dropped another ball, and making sure he flew the water, struck the shot too hard and a little thin, lining it over the green where he now lay five. After scraping his approach weakly onto the green, he two-putted for an eight. Discouraged and distracted, he double bogied the last two holes, ending up with an 85. It was a good score but a wasted opportunity for a great score.

Trudging off the 18th green, Andrew's depression morphed into his situation at the agency. He realized that he had been working and waiting all his life for the big job at WJR. He had read management books voraciously, attended every seminar offered, sat at Will's feet and listened at every opportunity. He worked on his presentation techniques and refined his effective management style. Every personal weakness he shored up in some way. He synthesized it all over a period of years. Finally, he put the team—the company—first.

Andrew was on the right glide path, but now a plane crash had dashed his hopes of reaching the top, just as a gust of wind had ended his chance for an excellent golf round. Now he was going to end up number two to Norman or Eric. He, Andrew, deserved better, just like the bad break on the 16th hole.

Well, he would just have to deal with it.

The protocol after the morning round was for everyone to ask everyone else "How'd ya do?" Andrew tried to avoid the how'd ya do's if he could. Who cared? As a long time golfer, and a purist at that, he knew that people really cared only about their own scores.

The people who had played well were willing to tell you hole by hole, shot by shot how they did. A few of those players who didn't play well, wanted to tell you all about it. He wanted to tell them, "Listen, Charlie, 80% of the people don't care and the other 20% wish it were worse." He never did.

One of Andrew's frequent playing partners stopped him in the locker room. "Hey, Andrew, I heard a great one out on the course today. What's the worst mid-life crisis possible?"

"I give up."

"That's when the golf game sucks and the wife won't."

In spite of his gloom, Andrew laughed out loud. "I'll have to remember that."

The jokester had a strong resemblance to Norman. He left the locker room and headed for the Jag. Before approaching the final corner near his house, he checked his voice mail at the office. A terse message at 6:00 p.m. Friday from Simon announced that he would be in the WJR offices at 11:00 a.m. on Monday. Shit. How had Andrew missed it? No matter now. The important thing was to get ready for the meeting.

Well, this is what he wanted. A chance to meet with the president of ENNU. He put in a call to Laura to crash on ENNU to meet the Monday deadline. So he had the meeting. Great. But he didn't have the foggiest idea what the agenda was.

CHICAGO, 1:15 P.M.

Eric had picked up some of Will's mail in his office after he checked the by-laws. Although afraid to pry, Will was still larger than life, even in death, Eric looked for any mail that involved clients, WJR financials, or industry-related correspondence that he might need to handle. The First Affiliated Bank envelope, marked "Very Confidential" was one of the pieces he took with him.

Now back home, upon opening and reading the bank's letter, Eric's first reaction was worry. That was a lot of money and the WJR financials weren't all that hot. If the incident ever became public, it could seriously damage the WJR reputation.

His second reaction was one of triumph. I've got the sonofabitch! This was Norman's responsibility. Norman's fault. This was a huge problem for the New York office. He now had a trump card to use...maybe even at the Sunday board meeting. The best of it was that Norman would have no way of knowing that his chief rival was holding this card.

If Eric could find a way to use it, Norman wouldn't know what hit him.

HAWAII, 8:30 A.M.

Awakened by the sound of the surf, Leon stretched out lazily and then reclined in bed, hands behind his head. This had been one of their best vacations in years. Great weather, good golf, excellent meals, new friends, rekindled sex with Diana, and nothing to worry about, except for this nagging WJR board meeting.

Leon sighed with contentment. He had needed this break. The consulting business was getting tougher and tougher. Every competitor had a process to sell and winning clients was becoming more competitive in ways that had never existed before. Rival firms were now advertising heavily–many on TV. Should he talk to Will about advertising? What was next...promotions? Coupons? He shuddered to think of it. But not too many years ago who would have guessed that consultants, law firms and hospitals would be advertising? What was the world coming to?

He decided to call Bunker to find out what was going on. Let's see, it would be 1:30 p.m. in Chicago. I'll call after breakfast in about an hour, he thought. He probably played golf today. Two-thirty Saturday afternoon would probably be a good time to reach him.

# # #

Breakfast overlooking the bay was one of their favorite times of the day on the Big Island. As they did each day, they sipped on their coffees and leafed through the newspaper. Leon was stunned as his eyes caught the follow-up story on the plane crash, with a mention of Will.

"Oh my gosh. That's terrible. Terrible. So that's what this is all about," he said.

"What's what all about?" said Diana.

"The messages I keep getting from the mainland. It's Will Raffensberger. He was on that plane that went down."

"God, that's awful. That was two or three days ago," said Diana. "How could the news travel so slowly here? "

"That's one of the reasons why we came here."

Leon sat for a while, staring at the surf. What had been a terrific trip was now a depressant.

"I've got to make a call," said Leon. "Why don't you finish your coffee. I'll be in the room."

Back in the room, Leon was unable to reach Bunker, but he did leave a message on voice mail. He decided to wait in the room for the return call.

CHICAGO, 4:00 P.M.

After checking into the hotel, Norman unpacked deliberately and neatly, setting out his wardrobe for both this evening and the board meeting on Sunday.

For the meeting with Andrew today, he had selected a medium gray pinstriped Polo suit with off-white shirt and red and blue patterned tie. He wanted to appear as the next CEO but not standoffish. This was to be a friendly meeting. Hopefully. For tomorrow, his most expensive, black soft fabric Armani suit, with white shirt and a subdued, sculptured, small pattern gray on gray tie, an outfit that projected the successful, powerful, New York advertising leader.

Having an hour or so before his session with Andrew, Norman decided a stroll down the Chicago lakefront was in order. It would invigorate him after so much sitting and help clear his mind. He grabbed a coat and headed for the elevator.

Crossing Oak Street and heading toward the beach along Lake Michigan, he walked past a small park across from the beach. Norman noticed two or three homeless souls with their plastic bags encamped in the corner. Interspersed with them were Chicago Gold Coasters walking their dogs and carrying small plastic bags. Maybe everything *doesn't* work in Chicago, he thought. You'd think they'd move the homeless on. This is a classy, little park; they sure mess up the landscape. Turning onto the asphalt walkway along the beach, he glanced at his watch and headed north, deciding to walk for forty minutes, 20 minutes out and 20 minutes back. As he strolled along the walkway, grudgingly he admitted that Chicago's lake with the adjacent Lincoln Park green belt was one of the handsome stretches of urban property anywhere.

The walkway was a mini-highway about 15 feet wide with a yellow stripe down the middle, flanked by two white stripes.

Norman was careful to stay to the side of the walk. It was crowded with helmeted bikers peddling hard in both directions, as well as tank-topped, flat-bellied, twenty-somethings roller blading gracefully along on this warm spring day. He decided that he could learn to like Chicago. Perhaps he should think about taking an apartment nearby. After all, he was going to be the CEO of an important agency in town.

CHICAGO, 5:30 P.M.

Andrew left his car with the valet parker and turned into the entrance of the Drake Hotel, leaving Sally to walk west toward Michigan Avenue where she planned to window shop while he met with Norman. Walking up the broad steps, he turned left toward the upper level of the large and elegant lobby sitting area and spotted Norman settled in the corner. Waving casually in recognition he ambled toward the New Yorker. Andrew noticed that Norman was dressed rather formally, in a dark gray suit. The Chicagoan was glad that on this occasion he was wearing his best suit, also gray, the new Zegna from Neiman-Marcus. A soft, rich weave, modified Italian cut, definitely a New York look.

"How ya doing, Andrew?" said Norman cordially, forcing his best smile.

"Things are going well, except for the Will stuff, of course."

"Yeah, terrible, terrible," said Norman feeling chagrined. "Have some tea?" He waved toward the silver tea service and pastry.

"Fine. Is this what's called Power Tea in New York?"

Norman laughed easily. "Close enough. It seemed like a proper thing to do on a Saturday afternoon."

I've been reading about the ENNU situation," probed Norman. "What's going on?"

Andrew's heart sank. How much did the New Yorker know? He managed to keep his game face on.

"Same old thing. You get a new guy in the saddle and you have to start over with him from ground zero."

"Anything we can do in New York to help?" asked Norman.

"Not really," said Andrew cautiously. "The first step is to meet with the new CEO, which we're doing in a couple of days. The campaign has worked beautifully, and I'm sure he'll realize that an agency change isn't necessary."

Norman wasn't so sure, but Andrew seemed confident that he had the situation well in hand.

Andrew decided to take the offensive. He leaned forward, elbows on knees, fingers pressed together.

"Look, Norman, I've been thinking about your proposal."

"It's more than a proposal," interrupted Norman.

"Well, it hasn't happened yet. In Chicagoese that means it's still a proposal." He grinned slightly at Norman to take the edge off his rebuttal. Norman grinned back warily.

"I want to know how you see the three of us working together, and what the vice chairman job is all about."

This is promising, thought Norman.

"Look, the concept is simple," he said eagerly. We split the basic tasks up. I oversee the new business program, Marcy has overall responsibility for the creative product, and you're the best client guy in the agency—you take charge of all of that."

"You mean director of client service for the whole agency?"

"The whole agency."

"But, you're proposing yourself as CEO?"

"Someone has to have the job. New York is the largest office. And the city is also the centerpiece of the advertising business. Makes sense, doesn't it?"Grudgingly, Andrew admitted to himself that it did make sense. If I lose the ENNU account, the New York/Chicago size disparity will be even greater, thought Andrew.

"You're not thinking of switching the headquarters east, are you?" queried the Chicagoan.

"Maybe we should have a dual headquarters," offered Norman, soothingly. The CEO/chairman in one and the vice chairman in the other."

"That might work," conceded Andrew. Obviously, Norman had thought this through.

Norman felt energized. "We'll keep rotating board meetings among all three offices as we always have."

Everything that Norman said was plausible. The problem was...could Andrew work for the New Yorker? He had never truly liked him, nor trusted him. Would this work?

"I don't know about Marcy being in charge of all the creative product. Is New York going to knuckle under to her?" asked Andrew.

"You may be right," admitted Norman. "It's one of the things, maybe the most important thing, we would work out after the board meeting."

Andrew glanced at his watch.

"Okay, I know where you're coming from now. Look, I have to get going. Sally and I are having dinner with the Hansons." He rose to leave.

Suddenly, Norman felt deflated. The Hansons! Had he failed to convince the Chicagoan? What would Eric offer him?

"Listen, Andrew, are you on board with me?"

"I don't know yet. All this is happening pretty quickly. I promised Eric I would hear what he had to say."

As Andrew turned to leave, Norman wondered where Andrew's head was at. For a few moments, he believed he had won Andrew over. Now he wasn't sure.

One more thrust. "Have a nice evening, Mr. vice chairman," said Norman cheerfully to the departing Andrew.

Andrew waved casually as he retraced his earlier steps down the staircase into the hotel lobby. Then it occurred to him that he had forgotten to ask Norman what his plans were for Eric.

No matter. He knew the answer.

CHICAGO, 6:30 P.M.

As the Millers walked toward the matre 'd station and the waiting Eric & Sadie, Andrew was struck by the contrast in the Hansons. He...beefy, blonde, affable, no Einstein. She...slender, dark, shrewish, smart. Was it true that opposites attracted? On the other hand, he was acquainted with couples who seemed as alike as twins (some even looked alike). He was never able to reach a conclusion whether opposites or alikes attracted each other. There seemed to be no middle ground.

"Andrew, it's nice of you to re-arrange your evening to be with us," smiled Eric affably. "How are you, Sally?" Hugs all around.

"What a lovely dress."

"How are the kids?"

"How's the golf game?"

"Isn't it horrible about Will?"

"I still can't believe it happened!"

The small talk continued as they were seated in one of Chicago's trendiest Italian restaurants. Eric danced around Sadie's chair to seat himself next to Andrew so the two men could talk during dinner.

The two ladies ordered glasses of Pinot Grigio.

"I'll have a Ketel One on the rocks, no fruit," ordered Eric crisply.

"The same," added Andrew.

"I didn't know you were a vodka drinker," Eric stated.

"Usually. Sometimes a beer. But it's been a tough week."

"The toughest," agreed Eric.

The women were chatting about Sally's children and Sadie's next charity benefit. She was co-chair. Eric decided now was as good a time as any to continue the courtship of Andrew.

First the flattery.

"Andrew, I've always thought you were the ideal candidate to run this company someday, after Will and I have moved on. You've got the total package. You understand creative, account service, every aspect of the business. You're probably the best trainer in the company, too."

Hearing the *someday* modifier, Andrew felt the depression he experienced earlier, although he was careful not to show his disappointment to Eric. If I'm that great, why shouldn't I have the job now, he thought? Should he suggest it to Eric?

The moment and the opportunity to make his statement passed, as Eric continued. "This is the way I see it happening. When I take over, I'll have to move to New York."

"What's Norman going to think about that?" Andrew couldn't help asking.

"He'll have to get used to it," said Eric sharply. "It's not like I'm a stranger. You know I've spent a lot of time there over the years."

Andrew knew. He also knew how Norman privately bad-mouthed Eric before, during, and after his visits.

"I think you're going to have trouble with Norman." Andrew suggested.

"Operation UFFDA" was hitting some snags. Already, Eric wasn't sure about Bunker. Now Andrew seemed to be siding with Norman. Maybe he had made a mistake not getting to Arness. Too late for that now. Eric doggedly pressed on, "I'll just have to pull rank on him then."

"I think Norman believes his rank comes from $250 million in billings."

Eric's mindset now was alternating between anxiety and irritation. Shit, instead of coming into his camp, the Chicago general manager was arguing the case of his New York counterpart. Maybe I should tell him about the Associated Bank embezzlement. Maybe not. Instead of trashing Norman, I'll pump up Andrew. That's what I came here to do. He switched gears.

"With you as the number two person ..."

"So you see me as the number two in the entire company?" interrupted Andrew.

"Right."

"As the number two person, what would my title be?" broke in Andrew, now completely on the offensive. Eric was certainly a lot easier to handle than Norman.

"Well, uh, you'd probably be president." Shit. He hadn't intended to get that specific, but Andrew seemed to have pushed him to make the commitment. What the hell. He wasn't sure about Bunker; now he *had* to have Andrew on his side.

"Probably?"

"No, for sure, you would be president."

Andrew's mood brightened. So that was the offer. President. It had a nice ring to it. Was president better than Norman's offer of vice chairman? Rather than the title, the important decision was being number two to Eric or to Norman.

"What do you think Norman will do?" probed Andrew. Had Eric thought this through? "You take the big job, I come on as president and Norman with half the company under his wing gets passed over. How does that work?"

"That's why I have to move to New York quickly, to solidify the structure and get a handle on the business."

"So, you're in New York and I'm in Chicago and the two of us are running the company?"

"Right."

"How long would you be in the CEO job?" asked Andrew. "You said earlier, you thought I would be next in line. When would that happen?"

Eric had not thought about this at all. Somewhat flustered, he answered, "I'm not sure. It's something we'd talk about."

Andrew sensed an opening. Boldly he pushed on. "Maybe we should think about my taking over sooner. Why not now? I could be president/CEO and you could be chairman."

"What are you going to have, honey?" asked Sally innocently, breaking into the conversation and allowing Eric to withhold his answer.

Andrew glared at Sally. "I don't know. Haven't looked," he said sharply.

Seizing the chance to recover his composure and formulate an answer for Andrew, Eric exclaimed, "I hear the tortellini is terrific."

The conversation group now became a foursome. Now Eric could deal with Andrew later. Eric was relieved. Andrew was anxious.

LAKE FOREST, 8:30 P.M.

Thirty-one miles north, Sandy Bunker cradled a glass of port with his left hand while making notes on his pocket note cards with the other hand. It was a rare quiet Saturday night at home for the banker and his wife, Margot. These were the nights when they caught up with each other's activities at cocktails before dinner. Tonight they also compared calendars up to six months down the road.

The Bunkers traveled together frequently on business, and with Margot's charity work and other activities, plus his business and civic commitments, juggling their calendars was no easy task. Sandy took care of all of the family travel arrangements and literally planned out six to nine months.

Having synched up their lives, the two enjoyed a quiet dinner. Bunker's mind, however, kept wandering back to the board meeting tomorrow and what the outcome might be.

Four hours earlier, Arness had finally connected with civilization when Sandy returned his call. Leon was sorry he had been so hard to reach, but this was a once-in-a-great-while getaway and he had also given his secretary the same time off. Yes, he was devastated about Will, but couldn't get back for the board meeting. However, he would try to get on the red-eye that night in hopes of getting back for the memorial services, if there were no weather problems.

Bunker had explained the situation concerning selection of the next CEO. Arness, being further removed than Bunker from the inner workings of WJR, deferred to the banker.

"I trust your judgment," he said. "Besides, you're the one to decide what's best so you can protect your financial interests."

"I have an idea, Leon," Bunker had suggested. "Why don't you fax me a signed proxy, authorizing me to cast your vote, just in case I need it. On second thought, the way to do this is I'll fax you a form and you sign and return it."

"No problem," replied Arness.

The proxy was signed, returned, and now in Bunker's WJR folder. He didn't know whether his methodology was legal or not, but figured none of the other directors present would know either. They were advertising people, not corporate lawyers. Unlike most boards, this one did not have a lawyer as a director.

Sandy sipped on his port as he began to list the anticipated WJR votes:

Norman	·Norman
Marcy	·Norman (says N.)
Hanson	·Hanson
Andrew	·Undecided
Bunker (plus Arness)	·Undecided (2)

Obviously, Andrew was a key. Scenario one: if the Chicago GM favored Norman, then Bunker could use his own vote and Leon's proxy voting for Hanson to cause a deadlock at three to three, Norman versus Hanson. Sandy could do that if he wanted to block Norman.

Scenario two: he could withhold the proxy and Norman would have the majority, three to two.

Scenario three: on the other hand, if Andrew swung his support toward Eric, Bunker could put the executive VP into the CEO slot by casting only his own vote. Then, at 3 to 2 in favor of Eric, Leon's possibly illegal proxy was not needed.

Scenario four: or he could also vote for Norman, swinging the election to Norman.

The net of all this was if Andrew went with Norman, Sandy could make that happen or cause a deadlock with Hanson, but he could not get Hanson elected.

On the other hand, if Andrew went with Hanson, Sandy could use the two votes he controlled to swing the election either way, toward Hanson or Norman.

So the real question in all of this was where Andrew stood. Bunker decided to try to find out. He called Andrew's home. Getting the Miller's voice mail, he left a message to have Andrew call him before 11:30 that night or between 7:30 a.m. and 8:30 a.m. on Sunday morning.

Sandy was beginning to lean toward Hanson. The Chicagoan might be easier to control. At least he was close by. God knows what Norman would be up to in New York.

Bunker finished his port and turned on the news to wait for Andrew's call. He had no idea where Andrew stood.

CHICAGO, 9:00 P.M.

As the dishes were cleared at La Scala, Eric—having formulated his answer—turned to Andrew to finish the boardroom conversation.

"Andrew, you may, in fact, believe that you can run WJR now. But think about it, as president you would already have a big say in what goes on in the day-to-day operations. In fact, I'd want you to run the business as chief operating officer."

"Is that the title?"

"Well, that's what it would come to be."

"How soon?" Andrew pressed. He was energized now that he learned that the burly ex-athlete could be bullied.

"Well, very soon. As soon as I could solidify the situation in New York. Look, this is all moving along very quickly. Trust me. We'll work it out. But the important point for you to think about is that you would move up in the company to an important–an extremely important–position. Now."

Silently, Andrew agreed. Even with Hanson as CEO, Andrew would be running the ship.

Having given up much more than he had planned, Eric circled back to reinforce his CEO status. "Andrew, you should know that Will and I had many private discussions about my being next in line. It's what he wanted." Andrew wondered if this were true or not. There was no way to know.

The Chicago GM relaxed and let Eric carry the conversation. Actually, he had gotten more concessions from Eric than he had expected. He had put forth his own candidacy and received promises about his future.

So the question was, vice chairman with Norman or president, COO with Eric.

With Norman as CEO, the three people who controlled the business could keep moving the company forward. With Hanson in charge, Norman would probably bolt, and probably take some business and people with him. It would not be good for the New York office.

Norman's election would be better for the company; Hanson's ascension would be better for Andrew personally.

Both options were fraught with problems.

# # #

A few blocks away, the restaurant in the Drake had been crowded and noisy. Yet another convention was in town, and a few of the patrons were still wearing their show badges. Marcy and Norman were able to secure one of the quiet tables in the corner.

They had spent most of the evening together telling Will stories, talking about how they were hired, how things were going in their respective offices. Marcy was upbeat about the upcoming presentation with Raul and Norman was appreciative of her handling and pre-selling of the Caesar's chief. Norman was equally sanguine about his next meeting with Associated Foods. Marcy even had a couple of good ideas for creative approaches.

They discussed Andrew's ENNU situation. Both had heard the rumors about the account being shaky.

"Well, is Andrew with us or against us?" asked Marcy at last.

"You know, I'm really good at reading people, but I really can't tell where he's coming from. What did you think when you talked to him?"

"I couldn't tell either."

"Well, I can't do anything else today," he said, glancing at his watch. "I think I'm going to turn in. Haven't heard a word about Leon. I don't even know whether he'll be at the meeting. A lot of scenarios to consider. Need to be fresh for tomorrow."

"Me too. Big day, Mr. CEO."

"Good night, Madame president."

# # #

Just around the corner, in the dimly lit hotel bar, Sir George made a few last notes while he nursed his last single malt scotch of the day. Having traveled all day–his flight from England was delayed–he was exhausted and appeared more rumpled than usual. Still packed upstairs in his room was the package of visual aids to present his case to acquire WJR, as well as handouts for all the directors. His visuals included the background of Helmsley & Hofer, a reel of their television commercials, and samples of the print advertising. In spite of his preparation and his well-organized presentation, the truth was that he was not at all optimistic about making the sale work. There were too many variables, too many unknowns, and not much time. Sometimes huge business deals were accomplished in a matter of days, but often the participants were known to one another and eager to deal. Obviously, this was not the case with WJR.

During their negotiations, Will had briefed him thoroughly on the WJR players: Norman the rainmaker, Andrew the cheerleader, Eric the athlete, and Sheena, queen of the jungle. Quite a collection, he thought, and each one undoubtedly had a different agenda and required a different approach. To get everyone pointed in the same direction during the first contact was the longest of shots. Was he a blithering idiot for coming all this way to confront all these obstacles?

Walking in cold like this, perhaps the best he could hope for was to plant the seed with the managers and hope to move forward with the acquisition in the near future, as soon as they became aware of the financial morass they faced and of H&H as the answer to their problems.

Sir George forced himself to buck up. What in bloody hell is wrong with me, he thought? I dragged myself across the pond to win over this agency and I can't afford to have negative thoughts. I know there are six surviving directors and I have a strong case for the two outside votes. Win any of the four insiders and at least there is a deadlock. And when there's a deadlock, maybe there's a chance to negotiate. Sir George downed his scotch and signed the check to his room.

CHICAGO, 10:45 P.M.

Eric left the dinner drained, not being able to think anymore about what transpired at dinner. He now faced another task, a particularly unpleasant one. Will's eulogy had to be written. That was not going to be easy. However, when it came right down to it, Will was responsible for some great accomplishments. That's probably what he should do—focus on what his leader had accomplished, then throw in a few personal anecdotes or two.

Writing a eulogy was like writing an ad. First you wrote a headline, then you filled in the copy and finally added a snappy ending.

EVANSTON, 11:10 P.M.

Sally pulled into the drive. She had strongly suggested taking the wheel after watching Andrew down several drinks at dinner. He gave in easily, remembering the events of only three nights ago. So much had happened in the last 72 hours, it seemed like a week ago. In the house the message light was blinking. It was Bunker. The last thing he wanted was another conversation that night about WJR. On the other hand, he wanted to get up tomorrow fresh and unencumbered by a list of things to do, calls to make.

He dialed Sandy, who answered after the first ring.

"Hello. Oh Andrew. Thanks so much for calling me back. Look, it's late for both of us, so I won't take your time by beating around the bush. If you don't want to tell me, I understand, but I do have to ask you...who are you supporting for CEO tomorrow?"

Andrew hesitated. Should be blurt out his own name?

"I really don't know," he said slowly. "I've had so many conversations about it today, I need some time to sort through everything. I just can't give you an answer right now. Sorry."

"Is there anything I can do to help you think this through?" asked Sandy. "Is there anything we should talk about?"

"Nope. It's something I have to do myself."

"I understand. See you tomorrow, Andrew."

"Good night."

Tomorrow it would come to him. He hoped.

Sunday

It was a relatively warm, sun-drenched morning in the leafy, handsome suburb as Andrew awakened. Unfortunately, he would spend a good part of the day closeted in the WJR/Chicago boardroom and then change venues to Will's memorial service. Some day. First his funeral as a rising star? Then Will's funeral.

Anything could happen. At least he, Andrew, would have a lot to say about what would happen. And at least he had choices, even if he had not yet chosen his poison: Norman or Eric. Last night he had hoped it would come to him when he woke up. It hadn't. Would there be a sign before the board meeting, or would he have to force the decision on the spot?

He shuffled downstairs anxious for black coffee and a good breakfast. Andrew always thought more clearly after beginning the day with an ample meal.

LAKE FOREST, 7:20 A.M.

Looking out at the morning sun shimmering across Lake Michigan, Sandy was struck again by the magnificent view from his terrace, overlooking the lake. This was Illinois, but he could have been anywhere in the world where green bluffs presided over sandy shores. He wished he could spend the morning sipping coffee and watching the occasional sailboat glide by.

Sandy was apprehensive about the upcoming events of the day. While he had something to lose, there was little to gain except the opportunity to somehow extricate his bank from WJR's problems over a period of time.

He revisited a thought that kept recurring ever since this mess had begun. Perhaps he should exert much more influence over the fate of WJR. If there was a deadlock (scenario one), maybe he should have himself elected chairman of WJR, as the ultimate compromise candidate. How else could the deadlock be settled? Perhaps the non-executive chairman of the board title, that was somewhat in vogue in the business world, would suffice here. He wouldn't have to leave his post at the bank.

As chairman, it would signal to his associates at the bank that he was taking positive action to protect the bank's interests. And indeed, as decision maker, rather than "advisor" he would be doing his duty to his firm.

And so the morning of the critical board meeting, Sandy Bunker became the dark horse, compromise candidate for leadership of WJR. But a reluctant one, at that.

CHICAGO, 7:25 A.M.

Sadie Hanson watered the plants in front of the tall tinted windows in the 26th floor apartment overlooking Lake Shore Drive. With a commanding view of the lake, the spacious nine-room apartment was professionally decorated down to the impressionist paintings that

Sadie deemed appropriate for an executive vice president of a major agency in town. For the first time, she wondered if they should move into something larger and more suitable for the CEO of WJR.

Not so fast. The deal was far from done, she thought, knowing that the linchpin of the entire process was probably Andrew. She and Eric had thought through the same scenarios. Of course, her husband would have to verbally advance his case persuasively during the board meeting. However, she wasn't worried about his upcoming performance. Although Eric was perhaps not as quick as some of his peers, he was a "big game" performer, a quality that stemmed from his successful athletic background.

Over the years he had learned to be an effective presenter; Eric had the knack of being able to relax and perform at crunch-time. His athletic carriage and imposing looks helped. But he had practiced the right techniques, too. In athletics he learned to take two deep breaths before shooting a free throw and whisper to himself "gimme the ball, gimme the ball."

Eric would be ready. But would it be enough?

#

Norman did not sleep well. He was neither surprised nor apprehensive about this fact because he never really fared well before an important new business pitch either. He was simply too keyed up to sleep much when he was faced with a vital presentation. Norman had been up since 5:30 a.m. and was expecting room service any moment—a light breakfast of fruit, yogurt and a bagel.

Today would be the pitch of his life. Could he win? Why not? He was New York Norman, from the center of the advertising world, controlling, by far, the biggest WJR office. He had the office numbers. He had the plan. He was the man.

He was bulletproof.

SUNDAY

FLAGSTAFF, ARIZONA, 8:00 A.M.

As the jetliner crossed Arizona Leon Arness attempted once more to nap. What a pain , he thought. You have a great vacation, get all relaxed and rested, and then come back tired. Sure he felt badly about what had happened, but he really did not know Raffensberger all that well. Plus, he was unable to make the board meeting, which at least promised some fireworks that might be worth traveling for.

He could only make the funeral service. Emily Raffensberger probably wouldn't even recognize or remember him. It was likely that he wouldn't even get credit for his return. Other than signing the visitor's book, how did people know if you were at the funeral service or not? They were always too preoccupied with everything else that was going on.

Oh well, you had to keep appearances up, and he was pulling down a $25,000 director's fee. Maybe he ought to make it a point to schmooze the next CEO at the services to make sure he held on to his directorship.

Now, with a goal to be accomplished, Leon's irritation and resentment began to melt away. He drifted off into a much-needed light sleep.

CHICAGO, 8:10 A.M.

Marcy pushed back the covers and stepped out of bed. She moved unhurriedly through her morning routine. There was little morning prep required from her for the board meeting. As always, she would deliver the standard report about what was happening in LA. She had old-fashioned overheads with her to explain briefly that all was well financially. Ever since the fancy smancy computer projection system broke down three board meetings ago, she shifted to the overheads. Besides the financials, she would spend some time revealing the two dynamite campaigns that would be ready to show the Caesar's client upon her return.

As for the CEO battle, that was in Norman's hands, and by to-night, if all went well, Sheena, Queen of the LA jungle, would be the new president of WJR. She supposed something could go wrong with Norman's candidacy, but at least for her it was not a win-lose situation, rather a win or status quo deal.

CHICAGO, 8:15 A.M.

Sir George finished his coffee as he ran through his presentation one more time. Convinced his case was well in order, he spent the next few minutes rehearsing answers to the anticipated questions.

"How will this global network really function?"

"Why did you select WJR as your U.S. partner?"

"What would the reporting structure be?"

He smiled wryly as he silently delivered the answers. No matter how many questions you conjured up, someone always asked the one you didn't prepare for.

Oh well, he was always quite good on his feet. Beginning to pack up his materials, Sir George felt he as ready as he could be. His hopes were not high, but possibly, just possibly, he could convince these chaps to buy into his plan. If not now, then soon.

#

One hundred yards away, in the park across from the hotel, Saturday's Chicago Tribune sports page covered Arnie Guerandt's face as he slept face up on a bench. The traffic roaring by just 50 feet away on Lake Shore Drive and the other sounds of morning in Chicago had finally awakened him from his drug-induced sleep. Flipping the paper off his head and tugging on the dirty, ragged army blanket surrounding the rest of his body, he sat up groggily and rubbed his eyes for several moments. Glancing down underneath the bench, he was relieved, as always, to discover that his meager belongings and winter coat were still in the plastic bag. His prize possession were the Air Jordan sneakers, now seven years old, but still serviceable.

Arnie had only recently moved to his "summer residence," the park land of Chicago along the north shore, where he roamed north and south along a five-mile corridor. In the winter, he lived below Wacker Drive amid the homeless village made up of dirty mattresses, moldy blankets and old corrugated held together by duct tape.

Even though the city had recently constructed prison-like wire fences to keep the homeless community out of the lower level streets, Arnie always found a space to reside. He didn't need much room.

Each year, when it was time to return to his winter quarters, Arnie fantasized about moving south to say, Florida. Why in the world would someone who's homeless stay in Chicago to endure the bitter winters? Unfortunately, he didn't have the planning ability, the transportation or the money to make the move. Besides, he lived only one day at a time, anyway. He could always move tomorrow, or some other time.

His daily existence was in a way prehistoric. Each morning when he awoke, his day was extraordinarily simple. Arnie was forced to hunt for sustenance and protection. Protection was a park bench and trees, or some overhanging shelter. In his case, sustenance was more than food. His habit came first. Today, panic began to invade his mood as he remembered that his drug supply was depleted.

This was not going to be a good day.

OAK PARK, IL 9:30 A.M.

The 80 year-old three story stucco house was set well back from the quiet street amid a row of other mostly stucco structures of like vintage. The parkway was lined with huge trees that formed a green canopy for the automobile traffic. The yards were large and also surrounded by equally huge trees. While not an avid gardener, the smartly dressed woman watered her flowers carefully, with an old-fashioned mottled gray metal sprinkling can, even though it began to look like rain. Emily Raffensberger was killing time. Approaching Will's memorial service with dread, her big worry was whether she would faint or not at some point during the services. She had agreed with her daughters to a small, simple service in the chapel instead of the large full-blown head of state funeral that Will might have wanted.

CHICAGO, 9:55 A.M.

Agenda
WJR Board Meeting

1.	Approval of April Minutes	Hanson
2.	Introductory Remarks	Hanson
3.	Office Reports & Plans	GM's
4.	YTD Results	Hanson
5.	Technology Update	Shimmers
Break		
6.	Election of Officers	All
7.	Other Business	All
8.	Closing Remarks & Adjournment	Hanson

Sitting alone in the dark-paneled WJR boardroom, Eric shuffled the typed and reproduced agendas, wondering whether to have them already distributed when the others entered or to pass them out as the meeting began. He opted for the latter. It would show that he was in charge and that he had created the agenda. Just as in an athletic contest, it was important to score first.

He reached into the inside breast pocket of his coat to reassure himself that the letter was still there.

#

Coffee and bagels were set out on the serving table outside the WJR boardroom. All the directors present greeted each other in the staging area before entering the boardroom. Normally, there was the obligatory kidding, the how's it going's and the clasps on the shoulders, and the pecks on Marcy's cheek. Understandably, today the mood was somber and the remarks about Will were uttered in hushed tones.

Just before they entered the boardroom, Bunker solicited the group's attention. "I have a surprise guest coming towards the end of the meeting," he announced.

"Who is it?" asked Andrew.

"If I told you it wouldn't be a surprise." No one laughed, or even smiled. "But seriously, it involves a proposal that will be of interest to all of us."

"Where's Arness?" asked Norman anxiously.

"He's been in Hawaii and won't make this meeting," answered Bunker.

Norman recalculated the voting scenarios sans Arness. Maybe this could be good. "It's 10:00. We ought to get started," said Norman. "You know we have to be out of here by at least three."

"How can we start without Arness?" asked Andrew.

"There is a quorum," answered Bunker.

"Where's Eric?"

"He's in there, waiting for us."

The WJR boardroom was impressive. Deep paneled mahogany walls. Luxurious deep plush carpeting in the blue corporate color. Large soft blue leather chairs. Highly polished mahogany table. The whole effect was a meeting room that looked expensive and consequential.

Eric had been waiting for them, and he had already taken the chair at the head of the table. It was Will's chair. Everyone noticed, but no one said anything about it.

Eric opened the meeting with a statement that Arness would be absent; although he would arrive on time to attend Will's services. There was a quorum present, he announced. He then stood up and very deliberately passed out the agendas across the table, one at a time. Norman wondered if he was staying near the chair because someone might sit there...musical chairs.

"Here's the agenda. I'm officially opening this special board meeting at," he glanced at his watch, "ten oh one."

After the motion to waive the reading and to approve the April minutes, Eric delivered in reverent tones a capsule of Will's accomplishments. It was actually an abridged version of the eulogy he had penned the day before. He then requested one minute of silence in Will's memory. As heads were bowed, Eric glanced around. Even though he still had no idea which way Bunker and Miller were leaning, he was elated that so far no one had challenged him as the acting chair. And he was delighted with himself for coming up with the idea of getting to the room early and commandeering Will's chair. So far, so good. He was definitely in charge.

"Thank you. Let's start with the office reports. Norman?"

Norman's report ran for 25 minutes, much longer than normal. Confidently, he emphasized the already good numbers he would be making and augmented them with the possible, even probable addition of revenue to come from Associated Foods and other new accounts. As always, Bunker was impressed with Norman's grasp of his business and very pleasantly surprised at his aggressive forecast. His delivery and mannerisms, however, were a little too arrogant for the banker's taste.

As Norman took his seat, Eric countered Norman's optimism. He arched his eyebrows.

"You know, we never forecast new business at WJR. We're interested in what you can take to the bank...no pun intended," he nodded knowingly toward Bunker.

"My numbers are very, very solid, even without the food account, Eric. Do you want me to go back through them again?" Norman snapped.

"No. No...let's go to Andrew?" Eric did not want to lose control of the meeting. "What's happening in Chicago?"

The Chicago report was delivered with unwarranted optimism— no major changes in the numbers were forecasted. Andrew appeared upbeat about the prospects for ENNU and deflected two questions by announcing the meeting with Simon and the preliminary strategy for retaining the business. Normally, the ENNU situation would have elicited more discussion. But not today; everyone was focused on item number six on the agenda.

There were no questions from Eric. He did not want to chance antagonizing the Chicago GM. The other two GM's were also silent; there was an unwritten rule among the office heads to not ask embarrassing or confrontational questions of their peers during the monthly reviews. You didn't want to make someone look bad. He or she might return the favor. In this respect, all the line managers were in it together.

"Thank you Andrew. It looks like you're going to end up on your feet with this ENNU situation," said Eric warmly, with a broad smile. The weak attempt at humor drew no response. Eric moved on.

"Marcy, what's going on in LA?"

"Spending almost no time on the P&L, which was not great, but okay, Marcy focused on describing the new Caesar's campaign, which drew approval from all present.

Eric then reviewed the year-to-date numbers, which were behind forecast. It was all Bunker could do to restrain himself. The agency needed a big influx of new business, or major cuts in costs. Or both. Maybe he would bring this up after the election.

"It's time for the break," Eric announced "Let's be back in 20 minutes."

Eric was pleased with his handling of the Directors so far. The meeting couldn't have gone better under the circumstances.

As they rose and stretched and moved about, Bunker decided that he had made up his mind.

So had Andrew.

#

As Eric headed jauntily towards the men's room, Sandy Bunker grabbed him by the arm.

"I need to bring you up to date on something."

"What is it?"

"When you get to the "Other Business" part of the agenda, a guest is going to join us."

"What guest?" asked Eric suspiciously.

"His name is Sir George Helmsley. He's an Englishman and he's bringing in an offer to buy WJR."

Eric jerked his arm away.

"Why in the hell would we think about selling?" he replied, angrily and defensively. "Particularly right now. What kind of a trick is this?"

"Will was on his way to London to do just that, to sell the company," said Bunker patiently, but firmly. "And the big reason was the financial morass you're in. We talked about it on Friday. Your operation report today wasn't so hot. And the balance sheet is a bigger problem."

Suddenly Eric began to view Bunker as the banker who needed to be appeased, rather than the director who needed to be courted.

"If you look at the revenue forecasts we just went through, we should be okay. New York looks good, LA is okay, and Andrew seems to have a handle on the ENNU thing."

"That's all well and good," answered Sandy. "But forecasts aren't actuals and you have a real estate burden besides. As both your banker and an outside director, I believe it is prudent—and necessary—to examine the possibility of selling."

They reached the washroom and entered together.

Realizing that Bunker was not to be dissuaded, Eric changed his tact.

"Well, of course it can't hurt to listen."

What the hell, he thought. After I'm elected, I can stall this thing off.

Bunker smiled ruefully at Eric's 180 degree waffling. He wished that the evp were a stronger person, the kind of guy who would stick to his guns. Oh well, he would be relatively easy to control down the line.

Washing his hands, Eric asked, "Where is this Sir George fellow right now?"

"Well, he's been holed up in Will's office, waiting to be called in. I figured no one would think of looking in there."

#

Norman lingered in the hallway watching for Andrew, who had bolted from the conference room as if he were a man on a mission. In fact, he was, and had taken the elevator down one floor, where he headed for Laura's office.

Finding her in jeans, sneakers and a "Taste of Chicago" sweatshirt, Andrew gestured at the papers strewn over the coffee table and on the floor.

"Looks like you have the ENNU situation well in hand," he grinned.

"Well, it's coming. Here's some stuff you haven't seen." Andrew studied the work and nodded his approval. "How's it going upstairs?"

"The usual boring show and tell. We haven't gotten to the big stuff yet."

"You mean anointing the new leader?"

"How did you know about that?"

"Hey boss, everyone in the company knows about it. There are even people betting on the outcome."

"What does the smart money say?" probed Andrew.

"As they say on the election night news, it's too close to call," she replied cautiously.

"Ever the diplomat. Well, I have to get back. I'm still planning on going over the track for tomorrow as soon as the board meeting ends."

"We'll be ready," she said confidently.

"I know you will," answered Andrew, once again pleased at her competence.

The exchange with Laura about ENNU served to somehow clear Andrew's head as he turned away and walked toward the elevator. We're going to save this business, he thought. Now he knew what to do in the board meeting.

#

Impatiently, Norman continued to wait outside the boardroom for Andrew to return. He had already collared Sandy for a few moments, but got nothing more than a "Looks like New York is on the move," from him. Very noncommittal.

Andrew approached him.

"So Andrew, is there anything we should talk about before the election? Your support is really important to me."

"I think we've talked about everything," answered Andrew. "Sounds like Eric is pounding the gavel. I suppose we ought to get in there."

After everyone was seated, Eric stood and called the meeting back to order. "The next item is the election of officers. Although I am the secretary, because I'm chairing the meeting, I'm going to ask Sandy to act as secretary instead, and administer the balloting." He pushed the blank sheets of paper (to become ballots) down the mahogany table. "This will be by secret ballot. Before we commence with the voting, however, I would like to say a few words."

Norman stiffened and Sandy looked at Eric with a quizzical expression. Andrew shuffled the papers in front of him. Marcy studied her nails.

"It's probably no secret that I want to assume the CEO post. But the fact that I both want and am willing to take on this job is not the reason to support me. I have literally grown up with this company...at Will's side."

Eric rambled on passionately about the trials and tribulations of the early days and his part in building the business.

Returning to the present, he continued, "I can tell you with total confidence that assuming the CEO post is what my friend and compatriot, Will Raffensberger, would have wanted. I ask you to honor his wishes and also remember that the advertising and business communities expect this kind of succession. I don't have to remind you that communicating stability at this time in our history, is critical," he stated, glancing at Bunker. "I have the contacts in the industry and I believe I represent that stability." His gaze alternated between Bunker and Miller.

"I can promise the general managers a great deal more autonomy than you have had in the past. I think you'll enjoy the new regime," he said smiling.

Addressing himself to Sandy, "In fact, today's unit manager job is very critical at this juncture of the agency, so while one of the GM's might be considered to lead the company, there's no question they are needed where they are." His eyes swept all three of the GM's. There is logic in his argument thought Bunker.

Andrew's eyes narrowed as he stared at Eric, who looked away. No mention of Eric's offer to him of the presidency.

"I think we can get on with the balloting," Eric said quickly, gesturing toward Bunker and the ballots. Sandy could you ...

"Just a minute," interrupted Norman loudly, rising and pushing his chair out of the way. He buttoned his suit coat and paused for effect and to gain the group's full attention. "There is another candidate to consider, Eric." He continued before Eric could answer. Hanson ground his teeth, frowned and sat down heavily. He noticed that his knee had begun to ache.

"Eric has made some interesting points about his candidacy." Turning toward the others, particularly Bunker, Norman continued. "But his idea of being CEO of WJR smacks of being a caretaker," he said smoothly. "Certainly he has contacts outside the agency, but running this shop is not about contacts, and not about status quo stability. It's about leadership." Eric sank further into his seat and his jaw tightened as he glared at Norman.

"This job isn't about schmoozing the folks on the outside, it's about firing up the troops inside. The CEO of an agency today needs to set the tone and the pace of the agency...to drive the business and win new business."

"With all due respect, Eric," actually showing little respect and continuing to look toward Bunker, "you've never run an office. You can't have a feel for what GM's need or what the troops want from a leader. Nobody in this company has driven the business forward the way I have grown New York. You all saw the numbers during my report earlier. The New York office is 50% of our business. Even more if some of the new accounts come in. "Addressing Andrew and Sandy directly, "I don't mean to sound arrogant, but I do think I'm the obvious choice to drive this company forward as the CEO." He paused for effect again, and then continued.

"Let me be very specific about why." He held up both hands (close to his face) so he could physically tick off the reasons. "First," looking directly at Sandy, "you can be certain that the new CEO is on top of...close to 50% of the agency's business. Sorry, Eric," not bothering to acknowledge his competitor, "but you can't say that. Two," pointing to his second finger and glancing at Marcy and Andrew, "as a general manager, I have a feel for your needs, I can identify what you do every day. I know how to support you. Sorry, Eric, you've never run an office."

Eric turned ashen. He had not expected this. Having rehearsed his own presentation, he anticipated some kind of a response from Norman. But not an attack like this.

"Three, we've all seen the numbers," working eye contact diagonally, but skipping Eric, "this company desperately needs new business. This is no time for false humility...I think the record over the years shows that I know how to win business for WJR. As Will and I often discussed (take that, Eric) the advertising business is an income business. And new business is the life blood of the income stream."

'Sorry Eric' was not necessary. Everyone knew Eric was not a skilled new business strategist.

"Four, this is all about leadership. This company needs a man in charge who is a proven leader. And you can't learn that overnight."

Norman ended abruptly, and quickly suggested, "Let's get to the ballots."

"Hold on," cried Eric, raising his hand in the universally recognized 'halt' gesture. Eric was about to commit a ruthless act. It seemed the only way to stop Norman.

Pulling the First Affiliated letter from his breast pocket, Eric unfolded it slowly. "I beg to differ with Norman's self-proclaimed image as the man who is close to his clients and who can drive the company forward. While he's busy driving forward, fraud is happening behind his back. Do you call this leadership?" He read the letter to the directors.

Norman was flabbergasted. That sonofabitch! How the hell did he get that letter? He jumped up and took command of the meeting.

"Look, this is something that just happened, but it's already taken care of. I'm meeting with the client when I return. Don't worry," he said, looking at Andrew and Marcy.

The directors stared at one another uncomfortably. There was no response to Eric's accusation or Norman's rebuttal.

Norman said no more. Just as in a new business pitch, you didn't try to say too much in addressing an issue. The more you said, the worse it sounded. All he could do is to hope his four positive "reasons why" over-shadowed this one negative.

Meanwhile, Sandy had decided his dark horse candidacy was a bad idea. Why would he want to take on this can of worms, even as non-executive chairman?

In fact, Sandy was not influenced by Norman's four-point plea. He had decided to cast his support toward Eric, in spite of his distasteful last-ditch expose. His decision had nothing to do with contacts or leadership. It had to do with the balance sheet. He would either manage Eric to make the financial decisions he wanted or he would force the sale to Helmsley. Controlling Norman was too big a problem. The man was too arrogant, too full of himself.

Bunker finished passing out the ballots and announced, "Please cast your vote for the CEO of WJR and fold your ballot twice before passing it down the table to me. "We do have a quorum, and we will elect the new leader of WJR."

Andrew, at last, was forced to make his decision.

For the second time that day, the room turned to dead silence as the directors voted, some quickly and some deliberately. The entire process took only two minutes, although it seemed much longer. The ballots were passed back down the table to Bunker who collected them and shuffled them several times in an attempt to preserve anonymity for the voters.

Slowly and ceremoniously, Sandy Bunker unfolded the first ballot and began to tally the votes. The other four stared at him intently.

"Eric Hanson."

"Norman Steinberg."

"Norman Steinberg."

"Eric Hanson." This was Bunker's vote.

Both Eric and Norman tensed visibly; the next vote would break the tie. Sandy was unable to contain his surprise as he unfolded the final ballot and read, "Andrew Miller."

Andrew tried not to smile. He had swayed back and forth at least twice during the morning. Ironically, it was Norman's articulate argument only moments ago for choosing a CEO with leadership qualities that changed Andrew's point of view. He just knew he was the most capable, the most able leader in the company. He had the right stuff to rally the troops during this difficult time. Since it was a secret ballot, he would vote for himself. This might be his only chance to put forth the candidacy, which suddenly seemed so important to him. Sure, Norman would have two votes and Eric would vote his own name. If perchance Sandy might vote for Andrew, a long chance, it would at least be a deadlock, and then anything could happen. It was the longest of shots. It didn't work.

Each director wondered. Who the hell had voted for Andrew? It was either Andrew himself or Bunker.

"Obviously, we don't have a majority," said Sandy, still surprised. "I'm going to give you fresh ballots. I think everything's been said. Let's take five minutes and vote again."

So Sandy had gone for Eric thought Andrew.

His depression was replaced by a surge of power. I'm not going to make it. I *do* have the pivotal vote. When I swing it to either Norman or Eric, it's all over. Three to two. Now he knew that Hanson's support beyond the evp's own vote, was Bunker. And Norman had Marcy.

He, Andrew, was in control.

Meanwhile, Bunker's mind-set changed dramatically. It looked like there were now three options, not two. He hadn't thought much about Andrew as CEO, but Norman's description of leadership fit Andrew well. Worth considering for sure. Norman's election had already been blocked. Obviously, Andrew agreed with him about that. Now if Sandy used Leon's proxy he could swing the vote toward Andrew or put Eric over the top.

He, Sandy Bunker, was in control.

Once more, he thought about Norman. The arrogance offended him. More importantly, the banker reminded himself again that moving the power base to New York would cause him problems. There was no way he could influence Norman, and the geography added to the degree of difficulty.

He could probably control Hanson, but the clumsy expose of that production fraud and his weak campaign speech were two strikes against him. It was apparent that the executive VP simply couldn't lead this company to anyone's satisfaction. He had no support from the general managers.

Sandy had always liked Andrew and his style. Glancing at him now as the Chicago GM marked his ballot, Sandy made a decision. Until now he had withheld the Arness proxy, but he wrote "Andrew Miller" on his ballot and also wrote Andrew's name again on a blank ballot that he labeled "Arness Proxy." He had decided to break the deadlock between Norman and Eric and put Andrew in as a compromise candidate. Andrew's vote for himself plus Bunker's two would project Miller three, Steinberg two, and Hanson one. Andrew would be the new CEO.

The compromise candidate was the kind of thing that happened often in American business and in politics. Bunker felt that the L.A. lady would probably go along with it, and hopefully, he and Andrew could bring the New Yorker in line. If not, too bad. They would replace him. With Andrew in charge, the banker could push the sale to Sir George sooner rather than later. Andrew would have no choice. No one would have a choice. That was the best solution for the bank anyway.

Again, Bunker collected the ballots, and shuffled them, keeping his vote and the Arness proxy together. Sandy unfolded the ballots.

"Norman Steinberg."

"Eric Hanson."

"Norman Steinberg."

The others were expressionless as Bunker thought, well, that takes care of the Norman, Eric and Marcy votes. Now, here comes the blockbuster.

"Andrew Miller."

It was Bunker's vote. Andrew was stunned. He couldn't believe it.

"Andrew Miller, by proxy from Leon Arness." Andrew went numb. It was now two for Norman, two for Andrew. Both Norman and Eric spoke up immediately.

"Where the hell did that come from?" shouted Eric.

"Why wasn't that used on the first ballot? It can't be legal," interjected Norman.

"It simply wasn't entered before, no explanation is necessary, and it is indeed legal," retorted Bunker sharply. He held up the fax. "I have the signed proxy here. It's necessary to break the deadlock. Let's finish the balloting. There's one more vote to be tallied. He gazed at Andrew, who stared back blankly.

Bunker unfolded the last ballot deliberately. The banker's jaw dropped. He looked up at Andrew. Then to Norman.

"Norman Steinberg."

Sandy was flabbergasted. Andrew had changed his vote and cast his ballot for Norman.

Sandy had trouble getting the words out. "Norman Steinberg, by majority of three to two has been elected CEO of WJR," announced the banker tonelessly. "Congratulations, Norman," he said with a forced smile.

Eric Hanson was incredulous. He retreated to a sullen, dazed silence. Marcy smiled brightly at Norman. Andrew was devastated. Having played the ultimate company man to vote for Norman and avoid a company wrenching blood bath, he had passed up the opportunity of a lifetime. He had voted for Norman to weld the unit managers together, instead of for Eric, where he might have more control. He had done the right thing for the company. And he felt terrible about it.

What in hell had caused Bunker to swing two votes from Hanson to him? He couldn't believe what had just happened. Neither could Bunker, who wondered what possessed Andrew to swing his vote to Norman.

No matter. It was over.

Norman rose quickly and began to speak, "I want to thank the people who supported me, "he said, looking at Marcy and Andrew and smiling, trying to contain his exuberance. "I do have a slate of officers to propose." He was ready to move ahead and passed out a one-page document with his slate of officers.

> Chairman, CEO—Norman Steinberg
>
> Vice Chairman—Andrew Miller
>
> President—Marcy Gallipo
>
> Executive Vice President and Secretary—Eric Hanson

Eric was totally deflated. He was also humiliated. Suddenly, the executive vice president had tumbled from the about to be next CEO, to the number four person in the company.

"In the interest of time, I would like to approve this slate by voice vote," stated Norman, taking over the meeting and moving along swiftly.

"Wait a minute," said Bunker, looking over the list of names and titles. "Doesn't this need discussion?"

"Normally it would, Sandy," said Norman slowly and warmly. But I've already talked with both Andrew and Marcy about their new titles and roles. They're both in agreement with my thinking. The rest of the officers simply continue in their same title, including Eric, who has been executive vice president and secretary of the company.

Bunker looked at both Andrew and Marcy, searching for any disagreement. He found none. Marcy was still in Norman's camp and Andrew was still in shock.

"Do I have a motion?" asked Norman.

"So moved," said Marcy.

"Second?" asked Norman.

"Second," added Andrew quietly.

"All in favor?"

"Ayes" from Norman, Marcy and Andrew.

"Opposed?"

No response.

"The slate passes," said Norman quickly. "Congratulations, Ms. president. Mr. vice chairman. I look forward to working with both of you."

Without warning, Eric gathered his papers, rose from his chair, glared at Norman for a moment, turned on his heel and bolted from the boardroom without uttering a word.

As Eric disappeared, Sandy took the opportunity to mend fences. "Since we still have a quorum, I propose to make Norman's election as CEO and the rest of the slate unanimous. Let me put that in the form of a motion."

The question of whether Norman had a majority for election was never raised. While he had more votes than any other candidate, he had only 50% of the total votes. When the election became unanimous, it became a moot point.

"I second that," said Marcy.

"Thank you very much Sandy. I appreciate that very much," said Norman. "All in favor?" he asked with a smile. The ayes made it unanimous.

The "Norman Conquest" was complete.

Without hesitation, the new CEO of WJR took over the board meeting in a confident manner. He did not move around to the front of the table and usurp Eric's (Will's) CEO chair. Eric had been humiliated enough. His only acknowledgment of Eric's exit was "I believe we still have a quorum. I would like to continue."

The next item on the agenda was "other business." Bunker rose and described the "special guest." Norman was surprised but not flustered. He had won the big prize. Nothing else today was important.

He turned the meeting over to Bunker to make the introduction of Sir George.

The banker made the call to the Brit waiting impatiently in Will's old office, and then briefly discussed the background of Sir George's pursuit of WJR, including the offer to Will, although not mentioning the dollar amount. Upon completion of his discussion, he opened the boardroom door to Sir George, who entered the room, nodded a quick greeting, and carefully placed his charts on the easel. Then he paused to shake hands with the WJR directors. Finding little encouragement in either their polite greetings or their distant expressions, he began to speak. As he glanced around at his audience, he sensed that it was a collection of individuals who had already been through the ringer and were preoccupied by the earlier events of the day. Bad luck. This was going to be even more difficult than he thought.

#

Andrew listened to Sir George's dissertation with disbelief and mounting anger, shocked that Will would conspire to sell the company out from under them. He and Norman and the others had worked their collective tails off for years with the understanding that they would somehow buy out Will at some point in time. And, in fact, the process had begun five years ago. Together the three GM's owned 15% of WJR. This company was their birthright, and Will had tried to peddle it to an unknown Brit.

In his remarks, Sir George stated that WJR would operate as an autonomous division of H&H. Andrew knew that this would not happen. Being owned is being owned, lock, stock and barrel. They might be autonomous until the first hiccup, the first bad year, or the first large account that was lost (ENNU?). But, if it appeared that WJR was falling behind the financial goals, the new owner would step right in. Besides, H&H was a public company and now there would be other shareholders involved, who would be concerned and presumably vocal about their investment. The autonomy stuff was bullshit.

The rationale for the deal was strategic, explained Sir George. The benefits were two-way. The British company gained a strong foothold in the U.S., while WJR for the first time would enjoy access to a worldwide network. "This kind of network is vital in today's world to help clients with global branding programs," said the Englishman confidently, sweeping the boardroom with his eyes, searching for support.

Andrew was unable to keep quiet any longer. He had nothing to loose. He was not running for office. "Mr. Helmsley (deliberately avoiding the Sir George greeting) this is all well and good if global brands do indeed grow in number. However, with all the talk about this trend, in my opinion, there are very few truly global brands. Levis, Coke, maybe Wrigley Gum and a few others. But, the fact that a brand is marketed around the world doesn't mean that it means the same thing around the globe, or brings the same kind of benefits or connects to consumers in the same way from country to country. Quite possibly, a network of independent ad agencies can offer multi-local solutions—the right campaign for the country—rather than one campaign for the world."

"You could still accomplish that with our network," proclaimed Sir George.

Andrew retorted, "It may look good on paper, but in a wholly-owned network it's hard to get cooperation from local managers when headquarters is pushing each of them to make their own numbers and handle their own clients."

"You bring up a good point, Mr. Miller. We certainly would have to hash out how the network might function, and how we could avoid that problem," answered Sir George soothingly. Andrew quieted down, but was not convinced.

After the Brit finished his formal presentation, there were a few polite questions from the WJR board. It was obvious that from the

GM's standpoint, an acquisition at this point was out of the question. While Sandy did have some issues, he decided that this was not the forum, nor the time. The board meeting had dragged on, and there was still Will's funeral in the offing.

"Thank you, Sir George," said Norman with a smile. It's a very interesting proposition. I think you understand, however, that the timing now is not right for WJR. If we were to consider this in the future, your company would be a leading, perhaps *the* leading candidate, for further discussions."

"Thank you for your kind attention and consideration," replied the Brit in his most courtly manner. "With your permission, I will keep the lines of communication open. Who knows what the future will bring."

Sir George quickly collected his charts and materials and Sandy escorted him out of the boardroom.

As they walked toward the lobby, the banker reassured his visitor, "I will make sure the communication lines stay open. I believe this is a very viable option. If not now, then certainly in the future. Possibly the near future. We can talk more at dinner."

"Thank you for the opportunity," replied Sir George.

As Sandy bade him farewell, the banker resolved to keep the subject open and explain to the unit managers the financial situation facing WJR.

Back in the boardroom, Norman waited for Sandy to return. He would adjourn immediately. Now that he had been anointed, in his mind, no other business was important. Besides, there was the matter of getting the directors to Will's funeral service. He reminded them of the place and time, adding his own brief remembrance of Will and his attempt to somehow follow in his footsteps. Norman pounded the gavel.

The king is dead. Long live the king.

OAK PARK, 4:30 P.M.

A light drizzle had been falling for almost half an hour, turning a very pleasant, sunny day into a gray day. The gloom extended inside to the church. The religious part of the service was complete, and Eric was mid-way through his eulogy. He was doing a very credible job; in spite of the trauma and disappointment he had endured.

As hard as he tried, Norman could not keep his mind on the services. His mood was one of total exhilaration. He had done it. The "Norman Conquest" was complete. Maybe his father would acknowledge his degree of success at last. Maybe this would shut up his sister-in-law, Mavis, who bragged endlessly about his brother Nathan's accomplishments with his law firm. Maybe this would vault him into the inner circle of New York agency chieftains, that group who punched each other's shoulders at functions in recognition and performed at each other's roasts.

Andrew sat up front on the right side of the church with the other WJR executives, a weary and now somber group. The funeral service seemed to Andrew to be like every other service...it was raining and everything started late. Strangely, no one seemed to mind that the service did not start on time, even though almost everyone there hoped that it would be over as soon as possible. Then all you had to worry about was what to say to the widow and her children at the reception afterward.

One of the troubles with funerals, thought Andrew, was that the dear departed was unable to hear all of the wonderful things said about him. Too bad it couldn't be pre-recorded while the deceased was alive to hear his virtues extolled. The real problem with funerals, however, was that the deceased was unable to respond and even deliver a farewell address. Andrew made a mental note to create a farewell speech to his loved ones and friends to be read at his funeral. Perhaps he should videotape it, maybe even add background music. Nahh. That would be too much. Maybe just write the speech and designate whom he wanted to read it. He was jolted back to the present tense by silence. Eric had broken down near the end of his remarks and was having difficulty continuing.

Andrew discovered that he felt sorry for Eric. In a very short period of time, the man had lost both his long time mentor and his stature in the company.

At the same time, Andrew felt his own spirits raised, a phenomenon that always happened to him at funerals. You always felt better after the services, particularly on those occasions when you emerged from a dark church into blinding sunlight. You always felt lucky to be alive.

The enormous disappointment of not getting the CEO job had drained away during Eric's eulogy. Why the hell did he want the heavy breather job anyway? It was nothing but problems. Everything he faced in Chicago would be multiplied by three. Three ENNU's in trouble, three embezzlements, three Billy Shipley's, three of everything, at least. Plus, you had to suck up to the bankers and God knows who else. Let Norman have all the worries. He had the time—no wife—and the drive.

What was important anyway? Being alive, for starters. He had a great wife, and his kids seemed to have their heads screwed on right. He had a good job, too. The new vice chairman of a major league ad agency. In fact, he wasn't ready for all that grief anyway.

Three, no four days ago, Andrew would have figured he would get a shot at the CEO opportunity in another five years. Maybe ten. Why take on that burden now? Besides, there were other companies out there.

Reflecting on the unbelievable flip-flops of the voting, Andrew felt a certain sense of satisfaction for having sacrificed his own candidacy for the good of the company. He, single handedly, had been responsible for heading off a bloody range war throughout WJR. Eric was the only casualty, but Andrew felt that had nothing to do with him. Eric was Eric.

Sally nudged him. "What are you waiting for?"

Sheepishly, he realized people were getting up to leave, and he hadn't heard a word of the rest of the service. What a strange zone he had been in. As they emerged from the church, almost miraculously, the rain had ended and the sun had come out.

Andrew's renewed sense of well being continued. Breaking away from Sally, he weaved his way through the black suits and dresses and caught up with Norman on the way out of the church.

"I'm in your camp, Norman," he said with as much warmth as he could muster. "But even though you're now the big cheese, I hope I can still rag your ass about the big apple."

"Be my guest. Listen, Andrew, I want to thank you for swinging your vote to me. I won't forget it."

"If you do, I'll remind you," said Andrew, this time with a genuine smile.

"Look, I'm heading out first thing in the morning. Tomorrow we should find some time to talk—you, Marcy and me—about getting the word out, inside and outside. We also have to figure out what the hell to do with Eric."

"It will have to be later in the day, after the ENNU thing."

"Good luck on that. I'll talk at you, Mr. vice chairman. We'll arrange a conference call, maybe tomorrow afternoon."

Norman felt terrific. The Chicagoan was on his team.

# # #

The reception back at the Raffensberger house was for close friends, neighbors and WJR directors only. The WJR contingent did not stay long. They all had agendas. After shaking all the hands, hugging where appropriate, murmuring condolences and encouragement, Andrew, Marcy and Norman moved on. Marcy was headed for the airport to get back for Caesar's, Andrew had called for a cab to take him back downtown to meet with Laura on ENNU, and Norman wanted to return to the hotel to work on the orchestration of the new regime. In the advertising business there was no time to spare, not even for Will. (In fact, Will would have understood.) Eric would stay with Emily and the family until the end. He had nothing to rush off to, and, in fact, had nothing on for the next day.

Leon Arness had indeed showed and offered Emily and her daughters his heartfelt sorrow. It was obvious from the widow's reaction that she simply couldn't place him, just as he anticipated. Jeez. He and Diana would have been at the Sunday luau now. He chatted with Bunker near the punch bowl, and received the update on the board meeting.

Sally headed home in the Jaguar. Her idea was to have a quiet dinner at the club with the new vice chairman of WJR. She felt it was just what he needed. After the ENNU meeting downtown, Andrew would take the train home from Chicago and get off very near the Club. This way he wouldn't have to drive home from the city after his long hard day. Over dinner, Andrew could relate the happenings at the board meeting. She was surprised how upbeat he had been after the funeral.

CHICAGO O'HARE, 5:50 P.M.

Marcy dropped herself heavily onto the leather barstool in the Red Carpet Club. "Absolut, rocks, twist. On second thought, make it a double," she said to the bartender. "It's been a long day."

What a day it had been. The voting had been touch and go, but in the end, Norman's plan had worked. He was a pistol. Jesus, was Andrew too good to be true? What a boy scout. Well, she would certainly be able to get along with him anyway. This was going to be fun without Eric in the picture. As long as Norman didn't turn out to be Attila the Hun.

Marcy started to make notes on her napkin thinking about her next encounter with Raul. Then she crumpled up the paper, sat back and took a long lingering sip of vodka. The hell with it, she thought. I'm going to enjoy being a president for a while.

Flipping open her cellular phone, she dialed Ethel's number at work. She had to tell someone. Speaking to Ethel's voice mail, "Well, doll, somehow I got myself elected president of WJR. You can order my new business cards, and yes, I'll be staying in LA. New York Norman is the big cheese and Hanson's at the bottom looking up. Just wanted you to know. See you first thing tomorrow."

CHICAGO, 6:00 P.M.

"Why don't we order dinner when we order our cocktails?" suggested Bunker to his dinner companion, Sir George Helmsley. "I know it's almost midnight London time."

"That would be very nice. Thank you."

Earlier in the day, Bunker had suggested the dinner in the event that there was something significant to discuss relating to the possible acquisition. Although this was not the case, the banker figured that even if nothing came of this WJR thing, perhaps Sir George would be in need of some financial backing in the states. You couldn't have too many prospects.

As Sir George ordered from the waiter, Bunker stared at the tablecloth. A whole weekend wasted and what did he have to show for it? Nothing more than a possible future customer in the Englishman. Plus, he still had this WJR financial mess on his hands, and now Norman to deal with.

For his part, Helmsley felt no better. A two-day round trip from London, a painful presentation on seemingly deaf ears, and now a dinner that was probably leading nowhere. Oh well, he was ravenous and Bunker was a pleasant enough chap. Perhaps he might be a source of funds some day.

#

Finding Laura in the "war room," Andrew loosened his tie for the first time in the day and prepared to listen. The war room is where

WJR Chicago gathered the work and the people necessary to make a pitch, either to clients or to prospective new accounts. Just walking into the room sensitized people to the fact that something important was going on at the agency. Careers could be advanced or crushed, depending upon how an individual performed in the war room while preparing, strategizing and executing the pitch.

Laura had done a great job in no time. The object was to rationalize a new campaign that was built on the existing advertising. It looked to be one of the best presentations they had developed at WJR/Chicago.

However, Andrew still wondered what the real subject of the meeting was. Did Simon want a new creative campaign, or a new compensation system? His team was ready for the creative discussion, he had better get himself prepared for a compensation discussion.

It was very possible that Simon's objective was to hammer WJR to reduce the commission, or perhaps even change to a fee-based situation. Andrew needed to be ready for anything. He could think it through on the train North.

He had time to walk and still catch the 7:35 train. That would feel good. He had been cooped up all day.

CHICAGO, 7:30 P.M.

Eric pulled into his apartment garage after the 22-minute journey from Oak Park. Neither he nor Sadie had uttered a word. In fact, there was nothing to say.

They had said it all when Eric had returned home to pick up Sadie after the board meeting. After stalking out of the meeting, he had walked all the way home, from North Michigan Avenue to the 3600 block north. Along the way he wondered how could he ever do the eulogy, how he could face everyone, how he could face Sadie? The last 12 blocks were in a light drizzle, but he kept on trucking. By the time he got home, his knee felt like hell.

He angrily explained the events of the day to her. Sadie was strangely quiet. Her only question revolved around what would have happened if Arness had been there in person? They would never know.

Finally, she encouraged him, "It's like one of your old athletic contests. You played as hard as you could, but you simply got beat. Maybe there was one point in the contest that could have been played differently, maybe there wasn't. You simply got beat."

She rested her hand on his shoulder. "You've got to get your chin up and get ready for the eulogy," she said gently.

Now four hours later the weary couple would pour their usual Dewars with a splash.

Eric and Sadie would simply have sandwiches at home in front of the TV and think and talk about what might have been. .

WINNETKA, 8:45 P.M.

It was a quiet night in the mixed grill at the Club. The golf season had not really rounded into full swing, so the crowd was light. The families had come and gone; the next day was a school day. Andrew liked eating at the club. He didn't have to make a reservation, even though they were encouraged to, and the matre d' always welcomed him effusively. "It's great to see you, Mr. Miller."

Andrew and Sally were seated at the "New York" table, which was near one of the windows overlooking the golf course. They called it the "New York" table because seven years ago, seated in the very same spot, Andrew had announced to Sally that he was "very seriously" considering an offer to join a large Manhattan agency as Assistant General Manager. Sally was shocked and depressed, although she masked her reaction with a smile and a host of questions about the job, where would they live, what was the timing. They ended the evening talking about the advantages of living in the East, seeing old classmates, being close to recreation and the like. Even though Sally ostensibly supported the move, two weeks later, Andrew turned the job down, deciding against the lifestyle change. Ever since, however, they still enjoyed having dinner at the "New York" table.

The waiter approached their table. "Good evening Mister and Misses Miller." He handed them the red leather-bound menus.

"The usual?"

"Yes," said Sally.

"No," answered Andrew. "Tonight I'll just have a wine...the house Chardonnay."

Sally listened as Andrew recounted the voting and his role.

"I'm proud of you for putting the company first, "she said, gently squeezing his hand. "I don't think anyone else in the company would have done what you did."

"Maybe no one else is as big a sucker as I am."

"You don't mean that."

"No, I guess not."

"You were just being true to yourself. Listen honey, you're the vice chairman of a big national advertising agency. And at a pretty young age. I'm proud of you. Besides, let Norman have all the grief of being CEO. You'd probably have to spend half your time in New York...you'd get me here some night at the 'New York' table to tell me we're moving there. You have enough to worry about with this ENNU thing."

"You know as much about the ad business as I do, don't you?"

"I wouldn't say that, but I do know a lot about the kinds of things you have to do and the stress it causes you. And me."

"Here's to less stress," he said, clinking her glass. Was he kidding himself? ENNU was providing all the stress he could handle.

CHICAGO, 10:00 P.M.

Earlier he had thought of calling his father in Florida to tell him the news, but decided it was too late there–the old man turned in early these days. He would make the call tomorrow.

Having finished an excellent dinner in his room, which included more wine than he usually had, Norman put down his pen. Throughout the meal he jotted down notes. Now he was too exhilarated to work on his ideas anymore. He decided to go for a walk on what had become a clear, crisp May evening. Just to calm down.

It was something he rarely did in New York. Danger lurked there on many of the boulevards after dark. Curiously, however, people who wouldn't think of venturing out on their own city streets after dark strolled fearlessly at night in cities they visited as tourists or businessmen.

Norman did, however, slip on a pair of jeans under his olive-colored Sanyo raincoat, the better to blend in with the natives. He would probably be mistaken for just another resident of the Streeterville neighborhood. Exiting the hotel, he turned right towards the lights of Rush Street, and he headed out into the night with a spring in his step.

# # #

Two blocks west, on a side street just off State Street, a tense and shivering Arnie Guerandt leaned against the building with a cigarette dangling from his lips. He was positioned next to a building corner behind the al fresco dining area, which had not yet opened for the season. The ragged, unwashed, homeless Chicagoan waited impatiently, knife in hand, camouflaged behind the concrete and metal dining area, which now functioned as a version of an urban duck blind for Guerandt.

The Arnie Guerandt story was being enacted at various other locations around the city every night. A need for drugs, leading to a need for money, often accompanied by violence.

As Norman walked briskly by Arnie's station, the glitter off the metal buckles of his Ferragamo loafers underneath his jeans gave him away. This man was carrying money.

The stalker emerged from the shadows. Quietly in his sneakers—he fell in behind the New Yorker. As he began to pass an alley, Norman heard a rustling behind his back. But before he could turn around, he felt a sharp, searing thrust in his back between his shoulders. Then another and another and another. He knew there were more, but now he could not feel the pain. The energy drained from him. As he fell into the alley and tumbled awkwardly forward, he saw something in the distance. It was a child in short pants pursuing a man in a dark suit. As the child moved faster, so did the man. The child could not catch him. It was he, Norman, running after his father along an empty beach. The day was gray, dark clouds were rolling in, and his father walked along swiftly, never once looking back.

Breathing in short weak gasps, Norman tried to call to him, to run to him, but he was unable to talk, to move. Now as the black blood pooled on the cement, he could not feel his pockets being rifled. Nor could he feel himself being dragged sideways down the dark alley. A shadow in sneakers flashed by him into the alley.

Norman tried once more to call to the disappearing man down the gray beach, even as the last breath coursed through his lips.

At that moment, his eight-hour reign as CEO of WJR ended.

Monday

Having another cup of coffee after breakfast, gazing out over the lake, Eric sat alone in the morning room contemplating his fate. He couldn't remember when he had been so depressed. It was worse than blowing out his knee and blowing the regional championship that night.

Only 24 hours ago, he was about to be anointed as CEO. Today he held the number four title in the company. Even worse, it seemed to Eric that he now had no job. Being Will's aide-de-camp had been a job, but now with no Will to assist, there were no tasks to accomplish. More depressing was the realization that there seemed to be no prospects for the future, at least with WJR.

Eric decided to not go in to work. Glumly, he surmised that no one would miss him anyway. He left a voice mail for his secretary, telling her he was not feeling well and would not be in today.

It had been several years since Eric had actually managed or serviced one of WJR's accounts. Even then, account service was never his strong suit. While he was able to establish good relationships with individuals at some clients, he was not a strategic thinker and was not adept at bringing clients solutions to their marketing or business problems.

Eric now saw himself in the worst position you could occupy in an advertising agency. He had no strong ties with any clients. He also had no definitive administrative job. And he had no following among the troops. He fought (brutishly) the new CEO and lost. Would Norman be a vengeful conqueror? Probably.

CHICAGO, 9:15 A.M.

After sifting through his Monday morning mail, Sandy Bunker returned to a letter from the CEO of Chicago's largest food company. The letter requested that the banker call to discuss the possibility of coming on the food company's board.

Once, not too long ago, Sandy would have jumped at the chance. The food giant was one of the most prestigious and successful companies in town. Surely among the other directors was a prospect or two for the bank. The director fees undoubtedly would be substantial.

Bunker put the letter into the pile of "A" work to be revisited later, although his inclination was to refuse. Even the directorship for a relatively small firm such as WJR had turned out to be a painful experience.

The banker felt that it would become even more painful with Norman ascending to the top. It was now imperative for Sandy to make contact with the newly elected CEO. Norman needed to know the state of WJR's financial situation. In spite of all that had happened in the past few days, the problem had not gone away. For the agency or for its banker.

#

Several blocks northward, homicide detective Ray "Ziggy" Griswald carefully examined the contents of the wallet. There was no money or credit cards, but a company health insurance card and the WJR calling cards for one Norman I. Steinberg were left behind. Sloppy.

Griswald stood two blocks from the taped-off alley where Norman's body was discovered an hour and a half ago. There was a good chance that this wallet was connected to that John Doe who was now on his way to the morgue. The only item found on the body was a Chicago hotel key. All his clothes were from New York stores.

Griswald's aide, Virginia Grabowski, had delivered Norman's wallet to him. It had been discovered in a nearby dumpster, during the initial stages of a thorough search of the neighborhood. Luckily, what might have taken days took less than two hours.

Whoever took the wallet wasn't real careful," said Virginia. "Took the money and the credit cards and maybe some other stuff, but left the guy's name. How dumb can you get?"

"So, we've got a wallet that belonged to a New York guy and a body nearby wearing clothes with New York labels. Pretty simple."

"Looks like this out of towner, Steinberg, happened to be in the wrong place at the wrong time," said Virginia.

"Yeah, a real unlucky guy," replied Ziggy. "Real unlucky."

LOS ANGELES, 8:30 A.M.

Marcy swept through the lobby, decked out in a sleek black suit with trousers, accented by a yellow scarf, yellow belt and yellow shoes. She called it her bumblebee outfit and sometimes donned it when she had something important going on. The ensemble made her feel ready for anything, anyone. Waving at Ethel, she breezed into her office and tossed her briefcase onto the sofa.

In the middle of her desk, two dozen roses greeted her. The card read, "Congrats, Madame President. Ethel et. al."

Ethel had followed her in to offer a congratulatory hug.

"You're the most," smiled Marcy. "Where did you find these gorgeous flowers on such short notice?"

"You don't tell me all your secrets. I don't tell you all mine," Ethel dead panned. "It's just terrific—you being president. But, what does it mean?"

"I'm still not sure. Norman and I are going to have to work it out. And Miller, too."

"Where does he fit in?"

"Well, he's a key guy. All in all, a good guy. I can work with him."

"What's his title?"

"Oh, I forgot to tell you. He's been named vice chairman. We're kind of a troika."

"Sounds workable."

"I think so," said Marcy.

"Is there anything coming my way I need to get ready for?" asked Ethel.

"Nope. I have to get my act together for Raul. I can't think about being president or anything else until I get through this Caesar's stuff. Let's get MJ up here and have her bring the creative. What time is the meeting with Raul?"

"One o'clock today. He's coming here."

"Good. Oh, remember that Clete fellow who was in to see me Friday? See if you can locate him. I want to talk to him about coming to work here. Maybe get him in tomorrow morning."

"You got it, Madame president."

Big deal. She was president, but so far nothing else had changed.

Griswald was perched on the corner of his desk, simultaneously talking on the phone and munching a tuna fish on whole wheat he had brought from home. He was back in the station as others had worked on the confirmation of the John Doe as Norman Steinberg. A 31-year veteran, Griswald had learned to never take anything for granted, but the connection of the Drake Hotel key found on the body, the fact that Norman was registered there, was nearly irrefutable when corroborated with the wallet containing his business card being found nearly.

The voice on the other end of the line relayed that there had been enough evidence to contact Norman's immediate kin.

Norman's brother, Nathan, was located through the WJR/NY human resources department. Nathan had been listed in Norman's personnel file as the next of kin. The reason for the inquiry to WJR was masked successfully. Norman's brother would fly into Chicago immediately to identify the body. He could probably get here by late afternoon.

Griswald took another bite of tuna fish and began scribbling some notes. Discovering who had been killed turned out to be almost ridiculously easy. He now turned his thoughts to a more difficult task, finding the killer. Maybe not, thought Griswald. This guy was so sloppy, there might be some good prints on the wallet.

# # #

Slouching on the dirty concrete park bench fronting Lake Michigan's boardwalk, Eric reflected again upon how far he had fallen. Last week he had been at the right hand of the leader of WJR. Presumably the general managers respected and feared him. Not any more. From the top of the world—or at least near it—he had now tumbled to a spot where he would be working for a bunch of yuppies who were splashing in wading pools when he was scoring baskets for

Wisconsin. Christ, they were probably all in high school when he was already holding down a good job at WJR. His self-image as the next CEO had plummeted to that of someone who was wondering if he still had a useful function at the agency. Now instead of fighting for the big job, he may have to fight just to keep a job. Any job.

Rising from the bench, Eric began to walk briskly along the boardwalk, hoping that an invigorating journey would help restore his energy and his will to take on Norman. It felt like it was the fourth quarter and his team was down by 21 points.

CHICAGO, 11:00 A.M.

To Andrew's surprise, Simon Slater showed up alone. Was this a good sign or a bad one? No way to know. Some CEO's traveled with an entourage and some didn't. Andrew went out to the reception area to escort the head of ENNU into the agency. He was of medium height, medium build, dressed in blue blazer and tan slacks. Casual. Confident. Acting like the client.

"Welcome to WJR/Chicago. We're delighted you could spend some time with us."

"Thanks for squeezing me in. I know you must be busy." Smiling. Could be a good sign.

"I can give you a tour of the office now, or we could handle that later."

"Later would be better."

Normally Andrew would try to establish some sort of personal connection; the Navy, college, sports, whatever. Simon's demeanor was very businesslike, however. Andrew sensed he should just get on with it.

As they walked toward the boardroom, Andrew outlined the agenda.

"I'm going to give you a little background on WJR first, then show you some of our work so you can get a handle on us, then we're going to spend most of the time talking about you." Andrew followed the one-third-about-us, two-thirds-about-you rule.

"Sounds fine," said Simon.

"Laura Forbes, who runs your account, will be joining us, as well as the two creative directors on your business."

"Fine." Still smiling. So far so good. Maybe this wasn't going to be so tough after all.

After introductions in the boardroom, Andrew took his suit jacket off and casually draped it over a chair to set the client at ease. Simon did the same.

Andrew's presentation about WJR went quite well. The atmosphere seemed friendly. Simon asked a few polite but pertinent questions and seemed satisfied with the answers.

During Laura's "Brand Review" the client president became more animated, and several times asked questions like "Why did you do that?" and "How did that work?" In Andrew's mind, Laura handled the queries very skillfully. This was going well.

The creative idea portion of the presentation also seemed to go nicely. Simon nodded at the proper places, laughed at the right things and responded with positive comments.

The whole presentation took slightly more than two hours. After the conclusion, Simon said, "Thank you Andrew. Thank you all. It's been enlightening." Then he turned to the general manager and said, "Could we go into your office?"

"Sure." Perhaps this would present an opportunity for Andrew to begin establishing a personal connection and to set up a lunch, or golf, or the next meeting.

They both retrieved their coats and carried them to Andrew's office. There, Simon walked by Andrew's sofa and coffee table sitting area. He slipped his jacket on and sat down instead on the chair opposite Andrew's desk. Andrew had no choice but to take a seat behind his desk.

"It's obvious that you have done an excellent job for ENNU," the client said.

"Thank you," replied Andrew, smiling and relaxing.

"But, I've decided to go in a different direction. I'm putting the account up for review, and invoking the 90 day termination clause, as of today." He couldn't believe his ears. He's firing us! He just spent two hours listening to us, and now he's firing us? Why did he put us through all of that? Or did he decide after he saw our stuff?

No, Andrew thought. He had made up his mind to deep six us before he walked in the door.

Simon continued. "Of course, as the incumbent, you're welcome to participate in the account review. After all, you do know our business better than anyone else."

"We'd have to think about that," replied Andrew tonelessly, still shell shocked by the announcement.

"Well, I have to get to a meeting," said Simon, rising quickly from his chair.

"Is there any way to delay this review for six months, so we can have an opportunity to work together, to learn about your particular business goals?" asked Andrew, grasping for a straw.

"I've simply decided to go in a different direction," answered Simon.

"Then why invite us into the review?" asked Andrew sharply.

"I feel all the work you've done for ENNU earned you that consideration."

"I don't want consideration, I want a realistic chance."

"Of course you have a realistic chance, or I wouldn't have invited you," replied Simon. He turned to leave.

"I'll show you out," said Andrew, recovering somewhat. There was nothing else to say at this point.

As Simon exited through the glass doors, Andrew turned and headed back to the boardroom. The creatives had left, but Laura was still there, gathering up the materials and waiting for Andrew's report.

"That asshole is firing us."

"What?"

"He gave us our 90-day notice and is putting up the account for review."

"Why?" she asked.

"I have no idea."

"Are we in it?"

"If we want to be."

"Do we have a chance?"

"How often does the incumbent ever keep the account?" asked Andrew.

"Hardly ever. Otherwise why would they have a review if they wanted you to keep the account?"

"You got it."

"Jesus, what an asshole," said Laura as the situation began to sink in. "He acted like he liked us, liked the thinking, liked the stuff we've done, even the new ideas."

"Maybe he was just milking us for everything we knew," replied Andrew. It was an all-too-often-occurrence in the advertising business.

"It's not fair."

"This business isn't fair. It's not the first time it's happened, and it won't be the last."

"What an asshole," shouted Laura.

"No argument from me."

His first day as vice chairman, and he'd just lost his biggest account.

And he didn't even know why.

LOS ANGELES, 11:00 A.M.

Marcy and MJ sat in the conference room. Television storyboards were strewn around the table. Each storyboard showed the visual flow of a commercial with the accompanying audio typed on each scene. The two women had decided which storyboards to show and in what order. Now they were discussing the meeting set-up and the preamble for the presentation to Raul. The key element of the set-up was the WJR "clutter reel." This reel consisted of brief clips from competitive commercials, which were strung together, one after the other. The competitive scene clips were selected on the basis of their similarity. Viewing this reel demonstrated the sameness of all the advertising—almost all the competitors were doing "bite and smile" campaigns. Person on camera bites into crispy chip and smiles at camera. By showing these competitors one after the other, all selling taste, using the same idea, it would set up the new Caesar's commercials which took an entirely new direction.

At this point, after showing the "clutter reel", Marcy would exclaim, "Raul, we can't afford to blend in with the others, to do the kind of advertising that mirrors what others do. To win customers in that arena, you'd have to outspend your competitors two to one. You don't want to spend that kind of money and we wouldn't recommend it anyway. While everyone else is zigging, we're going to zag. When everyone else is going south, we're going to go north. We're going to stand out, we're going to break out. We're going to eat their lunch."

At this juncture, MJ would take over and present the commercials to Raul. Later, after the sale, other WJR creative people would come in and show how the new commercials would be introduced to the trade. They would also show some introductory promotions to gain trial for the new blue corn chip. WJR was an integrated marketing communications company. They created more than just the ads. The promotions, the sales sheets, and the public relations.

"Have we thought of everything? He's as slippery as they get."

"I think we're going to blow his socks off, "said Marcy.

CHICAGO, 1:15 P.M.

Andrew didn't want to go anywhere. He was having lunch at his desk. Nothing tasted good. Pushing "home" on the speed dial, he waited for Sally to answer. She picked up the phone just as the answering machine message carried Sally's "and have a great day." For a while he thought it would be a great day. Now it was one of the worst.

"Hello."

"Hi, it's me. It looks like I'm not going to get there for the soccer game."

"Oh my. Danny really wanted you at this game. He's worried about losing this one."

"Well, maybe Danny will lose the soccer game and I won't be there, but at least Danny won't lose the ENNU account," he snapped sarcastically.

"What? You lost ENNU? I thought this was just a get acquainted meeting."

"The sonofabitch listened to our whole pitch, smiled, acted interested and then took me into my office and fired us." Andrew was getting worked up again.

"What did he say?"

"He said he wanted to go in a different direction," raising his voice.

"What does that mean?"

"How the hell do I know what it means," he replied angrily.

"I'm sorry, honey."

"This business isn't to be believed," he said .

"I know. And you did such a good job for those ENNU people," she said consolingly.

"I guess that doesn't make any difference any more. Look, tell Danny I'm sorry. And before the game get rid of those damn ENNU's I got him. Replace them with something. Anything."

"Well, you haven't lost your sense of humor."

"No, I'm serious."

"Oh."

"See you later."

"Nah. That's stupid. Keep the shoes. I'll find some other way to blow off steam."

He hung up and looked up. The Director of Human Resources for WJR/Chicago was standing in the doorway. He did not look happy.

"What's up?" asked Andrew apprehensively.

"Billy Shipley is bringing suit against us," he replied somberly.

"What the hell for? We followed all the guidelines."

"Not in his book. Claims his performance was not substandard and he was never given anything in writing to that effect."

"How did he get all this together already? I just fired him Friday," complained Andrew with a pained expression.

"There are law firms that specialize in these kinds of things. They just crank out the legal language from their computers and substitute a new name and a new number."

"What is the number he wants?" asked Andrew anxiously.

"The opening salvo totals about four million, including damages and lost wages."

"That's ridiculous. He was making one twenty five. What does our lawyer think?"

"Don't know, I've got a call in to him."

"Why didn't you warn me about this?" snapped Andrew, suddenly becoming angry.

"Sorry, Andrew. I thought I did. Maybe you just didn't hear me. Besides, I just told you what they wanted...they haven't won the case. In fact, most of these cases drag on and are settled out of court for a lot less."

"How much less?"

"There's no way to guess at this point."

Andrew realized there was nothing more to be done until the WJR lawyer rendered an opinion.

"Okay, stay in touch," he said wearily.

As his HR director closed the door behind him, Andrew could only laugh ruefully. There were times when no matter how well you planned everything, how good a job you did, your world just turned to shit anyway. There was nothing to be done about it except to keep your wits about you and not lose your sense of humor. You just had to ride it out and wait until your world turned around again.

What could possibly happen next, Andrew wondered.

NEW YORK, 4:45 P.M.

Nathan Steinberg had arrived in Chicago by mid-afternoon and had made a positive identification of Norman's body. Immediately, he located a phone and called Ft. Lauderdale, Florida to break the devastating news to their father. Next he called his wife. Having taken care of family matters, he called WJR/New York to notify Norman's company of his untimely death. Unable to speak with anyone who claimed to be in charge, he finally located the director of human resources, the first WJR employee to hear the shocking news.

Being unaware of the Sunday Board action, the HR head attempted to locate Eric Hanson -as the senior officer of WJR—in Chicago. Hearing that Eric was taking the day off, he decided to try and reach him at home. This was indeed a matter of life and death.

CHICAGO, 4:05 P.M.

After the phone call from New York, Eric had trouble focusing on what had happened. . First Will and now Norman. He couldn't believe it. Norman, the source of yesterday's bitter defeat, was gone.

"Sadie," he called, "come in here."

"I'm busy, what do you want?" she said entering.

"Norman has been killed."

"What! You can't be serious."

"It's true. He was killed out on the street last night. A mugging or robbery or something."

"How did you find that out?"

"I got a call from our human resource guy in New York. He said he was calling me as the senior officer in the company. He heard it from Norman's brother, who identified the body here."

"How did Norman's brother get to Chicago?"

"It doesn't matter."

Sadie sat down and looked intently at Eric. "What does this mean?"

"I don't know, I just heard the news."

"Well, think about it. Who's in charge of the company?"

"I didn't like him at all," said Eric. "But I sure didn't want something like this to happen."

"Of course you didn't," she said. "But it's happened, so what do you do now? I'm asking you, who's in charge of the company?"

"I'm not sure. Technically, Marcy is president and Andrew is vice chairman. But there's no chairman/CEO now."

"Why not make another run at the top?"

"What?"

"Why not try again," she said slowly.

"I don't know. I can't focus."

Sadie continued. "Listen, just yesterday someone edged you out for the top job. Now, unfortunately, he's gone. It's horrible and we'll never get over it—just like Will. But the job is open and someone needs to fill it. The company can't be without a leader."

"Technically, I finished third," he said hesitantly. "Andrew got two votes."

"For Christ sakes," Sadie said. "Get your act together. You couldn't get it done the first time, but this is incredible. Think of it. If there's another election, at least you've got another chance."

"Well, let's see. This means there are five surviving directors. Arness is back in town so there would be five people involved if there is another board meeting and another vote."

"So maybe you should call another special meeting. You did it once—you're still secretary—you can do it again. Besides, didn't

Bunker vote your way in the first go round? If you can get him again, and if you can get Arness on your side, you're in."

Eric brightened. "You're right. Someone has to do something. I swung Bunker my way once. Maybe I can do it again. Why not Arness, too?"

From the depths of depression, after a crushing defeat, the ex-athlete bounced back to compete again.

CHICAGO, 4:15 P.M.

Sandy Bunker's secretary uncharacteristically interrupted a staff meeting in the conference area of his office.

"Eric Hanson of WJR needs to talk to you."

"I can't talk to him now," he answered, frowning and waving her away.

"He says it's urgent. Says to tell you something terrible has happened to someone called Norman."

"Okay, okay." Looking at his staffers, "give me 10 minutes and then we'll finish this up."

He rose from the conference table, moved to his desk chair and picked up the phone. He was annoyed.

"Eric, what's this about Norman?"

"He's been killed, murdered outside his hotel last night."

"What? Murdered? Are you sure? How do you know this?"

"I'm sure. His brother flew in from New York to identify the body."

"How did it happen?"

"I don't know," answered Eric. "What I've heard is that it was probably robbery."

"It's unbelievable," replied Bunker. "Coming on the heels of Will's crash. I've never heard of anything like this."

"Look, Sandy, it is terrible what's happened. But I have to move on this quickly. I'm going to call another board meeting to have another vote for the chairmanship."

"Hold it!" interrupted Sandy. *"Don't you have any respect for the dead?"*

"Of course I do, but this company is going to be thrown into chaos. Somebody has to take charge."

"I don't even want to talk about it now," snapped the banker. "I have to let this sink in." He hung up.

"The meeting is over," he said to his staffers.

Here we go again. Hanson making a play for the top. I just don't have any confidence in him, he thought. Here I am faced with being the kingmaker again. This company, with its financial mess, and its power struggles, just won't go away.

CHICAGO, 4:45 P.M.

Andrew slumped in his office chair in a trance. It had been 15 minutes since hearing the news about Norman from his director of human resources, who heard from his New York counterpart.

It was not to be believed that all that had happened within his company could occur in such a short period of time. His brain seemed numb, and he couldn't focus. What happens now? What's going to happen to the company? Who's in charge?

Slowly, it dawned on Andrew that maybe he was in charge. As vice chairman, he now carried the number two title in the company. Reaching down, he unlocked his lower file drawer, then pulled out the copy of the WJR by-laws. He had removed the leather bound book from Will's office at the first opportunity after his meeting with Norman and the offer of his vice chairmanship. The by-laws indeed had a description of the duties of the post. Andrew's head was clearing.

Revisiting the by-laws revealed what Andrew was looking for. "IN THE ABSENCE OR INCAPACITATION OF THE CHAIRMAN, THE VICE CHAIRMAN SHALL FUNCTION TEMPORARILY AS CHAIRMAN OF THE COMPANY."

Norman was both absent and incapacitated. There was no question that he, Andrew, was now chairman of the company. *Temporarily.* Why couldn't that be as long as he wanted?

Andrew found "OFFICERS. SECTION G." in the by-laws.

"THE OFFICERS OF THE CORPORATION SHALL HOLD OFFICE UNTIL THEIR SUCCESSORS ARE CHOSEN AND QUALIFY IN THEIR STEAD. IF THE OFFICE OF ANY OFFICER BECOMES VACANT FOR ANY REASON, THE VACANCY SHALL BE FILLED BY THE BOARD OF DIRECTORS."

There was no stipulation of when this had to be done.

So there was no requirement to elect new directors—who elected new officers—until the next annual meeting in April. As vice chairman, maybe he could name himself CEO. So, he would not have to go through another election unless a special board meeting was called.

He would not call it.

As acting chairman, he would run the company until the annual meeting, next April, 11 months away. By then, he anticipated, if things were going reasonably well, he could go through the formality of making things permanent.

Now what? His only possible competition would be Eric. What would or could the executive vice president do? Technically, he reported to Andrew. Plus, he had no support. Even Bunker had voted for Andrew–not Eric–on the last ballot.

The first thing to do would be to call Marcy and get her on board. Shouldn't be any problem there. Then he needed to talk to Laura. He would have to send her east to take over the New York office. She was clearly the best person in the company, talent-wise, to take over this task. She was also probably the best person to pick up the reins on the Associated Foods pitch that Norman talked about.

The New Yorkers might give Laura—and him—all sorts of grief over his selection, but he had to be bold. New York and the entire company were in turmoil. This was the time to act, to take charge, otherwise they would all flounder.

Next, he needed to tell Bunker what he was doing and ask him to get to Arness. They probably wouldn't fight it. Now what about Eric? He could use Eric's help, but if the evp didn't want to play ball, Andrew would move on. He was making notes now, listing tasks by priority.

One of his most important initiatives would be to manage the news, both inside and outside. But first, the conversation with Laura. He picked up the phone. "Laura, I need to talk to you." Come in, in about 20 minutes."

The phone rang.

"This is Andrew."

"Andrew, this is Eric. I have some terrible, terrible news for..."

"You mean about Norman?"

"Yes, you heard?"

"Yes... just a short while ago."

"It's awful, but look, Andrew, as bizarre as it sounds, I want to call another special meeting. We need to have another election."

"No we don't," said Andrew firmly.

"Don't what?"

"We don't need a special board meeting and we don't need a special election. Our officers are in place and we can go until the next annual meeting."

"But that's another eleven months from now," said Eric desperately.

"Precisely," replied Andrew calmly.

"Look, the by-laws say..."

"I know exactly what they say," cut in Andrew. "I have them in front of me and I'm going to read you the sections that allow me, make that *require* me, to assume the chairmanship." Andrew read the by-laws to Eric.

"I am going to assume the chairmanship, effective immediately."

"You can't do that," shouted Eric.

"I can do that. And I *am* doing that," Andrew replied very deliberately and calmly. "You can call a meeting, but no one will show. I won't and Marcy won't and I'll bet you that Bunker and Arness won't show either. You won't have a quorum."

Suddenly, Eric's braggadocio crumbled under Andrew's resolve. "Are you sure what you're doing is legal?"

"I'm sure." Andrew wasn't totally sure, but he was not about to back down now. "I've read the by-laws carefully. Look, I have a lot of arrangements to make. I have to go. But Eric ..." his tone warmed, "In my mind, you'll have a role to play in the future."

"What do you mean?"

"So much has happened, with losing Will and Norman, we need to project as much stability as possible."

"What do you have in mind?"

"Look, I can't talk now, but you are probably the best man to visit all the offices and tell them where we go from here."

"Where do we go from here?" asked Eric.

"I've already put together some ideas. I'll get them to you soon."

"Okay. Well, I'll let you go," replied Eric, now deflated and defeated again. But there was a ray of hope. "Maybe we can talk about my role tomorrow?"

"Sure, maybe over lunch."

Andrew hung up. He had no ideas for Eric. But he would by the time they had lunch tomorrow. He checked his written list. Now he had better get to Marcy and Bunker.

He wondered what Bunker would say.

LOS ANGELES, 3:00 P.M.

Marcy relaxed in her office after showing Raul out. The presentation had gone extremely well. He had liked both campaigns and was also on board with the promotion ideas and the trade program. Of course, he found one flaw in the mechanics of the promotion program and complained about the high cost of everything, particularly producing the television commercials. He always found something—you couldn't let the agency believe they knew all the answers, could you?

This was fine with Marcy. She always found a way to acknowledge Raul's often insightful comments and incorporate the changes into the campaign that would be produced. You always had to let the client win a few small battles on the way to winning the war.

The phone rang. It was Andrew.

The euphoria from this big win, coming on top of her ascension to the presidency drained away almost instantly as Andrew broke the news about Norman.

This was different than Will. Worse than Will.

She felt a real sense of personal loss, having really liked the New York GM.

From his tone and approach, it sounds like Miller's already in charge. And it sounds like he wants me to still be the president. At least not much would change in California.

EVANSTON, IL 5:30 P.M.

His driver deftly executed a hard right turn and moved ahead of two other cars. Bunker nodded in approval and recaptured his train of thought. The WJR problem just wouldn't go away.

Perhaps the only good thing that could come of this latest WJR tragedy would be the emergence of Andrew as the new agency leader. The Chicago GM had handled himself awfully well through the whole election process, including giving himself up to Norman's candidacy for the good of the company. The mark of a leader.

Bunker had pledged his support during their conversation one half hour ago.

There was no question that he would be able to work better in concert with the Chicagoan than he would have with the New Yorker.

# # #

Today the new chairman of WJR was facing a lot of landmines. WJR/Chicago had just lost its biggest account, the numbers outlook was bleak and a disgruntled employee was suing him. LA was trying to sell two new campaigns to a tough hombre. New York had an important client up in arms about possible fraud and a big pitch coming up that was probably going to cost a ton of money. Plus, he had to worry about sending Chicago's Laura Forbes into the Big Apple to run the New York office, and who was going to replace her–and himself, in Chicago? Not to mention the financial stress alluded to by Sandy Bunker that was now part of his life.

And that was just the stuff he knew about. God only knew what else was going on at the three locations of WJR that he wasn't aware of. Well, this is what he always wanted. Wasn't it?

Tuesday

It was the earliest Andrew had been in the office in some time. Now after an hour, his communiqué to the staff was on his computer screen completed.

To:	**Staff**
From:	**Andrew Miller**
Subject:	**Norman Steinberg**

It is with extreme sadness that I tell you that Norman Steinberg, the newly elected chairman/CEO of WJR was tragically slain in Chicago two nights ago during an apparent robbery. His senseless death is a terrible loss to me personally and to the company as a whole.

As many of you have learned, at last Sunday's WJR board meeting, Norman was elected by the directors to the position of chairman/CEO. He would have been a tremendous leader for this company and we will mourn his loss for some time to come. Our hearts go out to his family and friends and his associates at WJR/New York.

At the same board meeting, I was fortunate enough to be elected as vice chairman, and Marcy Gallipo was made president, with Eric Hanson continuing as executive vice president.

According to the by-laws of WJR, in the event of incapacitation of the chairman, the vice chairman assumes the chairmanship of the company. It is with great regret that I take the reins of this company as chairman/CEO. In spite of all that has happened in the last few days, the company must move forward—there are challenges to be confronted and opportunities to be exploited and clients who depend upon us to help them succeed in the marketplace.

I will continue as general manager of Chicago, and I am appointing Laura Forbes as executive vice president, general manager of New York. She will relocate immediately.

As we mourn Norman on the heels of our loss of Will Raffensberger, this is the time for all of us to pull together as never before. I know I can count on each and every one of you and that WJR will move forward because of your efforts.

My door is open to all of you.

He moved the cursor to "send" and clicked.
Andrew Miller was in charge.

Epilogue

ONE YEAR LATER

THE RIPPLE EFFECT

by Nelson Ripple

Many of you may recall that four years ago, three senior executives of BSB&R died tragically along with two clients in a back country avalanche in Colorado. But the two violent deaths a year ago that claimed two CEO's of WJR in less than a week was just as incredible and debilitating to this mid-size, Midwestern-based ad agency. Losing its founder and namesake in a plane crash and then the murder in the Chicago night of his newly chosen successor, New Yorker, Norman Steinberg, all within one week was shocking. Then its termination of the ENNU account (in this columnist's opinion, the sparkling ENNU work did not warrant getting the boot), followed by the loss of the WJR/New York bank business, cast serious doubts about the future of this agency.

This is a tough business, and when leadership is uncertain, the natives get restless. So do the clients, and so do the people. When Andrew Miller, Chicago general manager emerged with the job, the naysayers predicted he would fall on his boy-next-door face, particularly after the defections of two top level people–Marcy Gallipo in L.A. and Laura Forbes, who left WJR/NY and returned to Chicago. However, the new CEO managed to recapture ENNU and reel in a fair amount of other new business, as well. It appears that the young Mr. Miller, former Dartmouth oarsman, has been able to get all of WJR rowing together again.

And now he's crossed the finish line ahead of some of his independent agency competitors by engineering a brilliant merger with the venerable Helmsley and Hofer in London, adding H&H's global network to WJR/North America. Rumor has it that Miller is in line to be vice chairman of H&H, and maybe more down the road.

It's reassuring to see one of the really good guys make it in this most capricious business.

LONDON, 8:00 P.M.

June in London was a special time in a special place. Sir George wanted them to see it all–the back-to-back events–Cricket test matches, Ascot races, Wimbledon. Andrew and Sally relished the whole experience. They particularly enjoyed the long walks through the city from their hotel in Mayfair all the way to Harrods and back.

They had arrived in London three days ago, driving down from the Cotswolds. Andrew had rented a car at Heathrow and they had simply taken off. It was a marvelous four days for both of them. It had been years since they had done anything like it. The final two nights were spent at a 13th century manor, then on to London.

Andrew was engaged in a round of meetings with Sir George Helmsley. The subject was merging the two companies. While Andrew had been there several times in recent weeks, this time he brought Sally. She was thrilled.

Tonight they were eating in at the hotel. The waiter had just poured their wine (Andrew no longer drank the hard stuff.)

"So, now what do you think, Mr. CEO, after a year?" The last year had been such a blur; they had not yet taken much time to talk through what they had lived through.

"You know I was wrong about thinking that everything would be multiplied by three. It's exponential. Everything seems multiplied by nine! And it sure isn't going to get any easier. We'll keep winning and losing accounts and people. Nothing's going to change."

"Well, what's the headline? Has it been the best year of your business career or the worst?"

"Both," he answered with a chuckle.

"So which is which?" she asked.

"Well, the worst was the New York bank firing us. We deserved it. That was two million a year down the drain, besides having to pay off the money that turkey took."

"The thing that surprised me most was Laura Forbes not making it there," said Sally.

"Yeah, me too. When her husband didn't move, I started to worry."

"But he's a broker for a firm with a New York office. He could have moved, couldn't he?"

"Right, that's why I started to worry. She just couldn't hack it there, and without her other half, maybe she just didn't want to tough it out."

"But to go with your biggest competitor in Chicago."

"Yeah, that hurts."

"Are you still surprised at what Marcy did?" asked Sally.

"I am. And I'm still pissed that I flew all the way out to L.A. to give her the New York job, and she quits before I can even set up the offer. God, those dot com companies are nuts–they doubled her salary!"

"Well, how is that JM?"

"MJ!"

"Right, how is that MJ doing in LA?"

"Really well. She was the creative director, and creative is what it's all about out there. So far, so good. L.A. is okay. That's why we still have the Caesar's business and the creative work is pretty good."

"So what about trying to get Marcy's advertising account?" asked Sally.

"Not likely. Ex-employees make the worst clients. They know too much about everything that's wrong with you."

"So what are you worried most about right now?"

"Well, that Billy Shipley business. It's unbelievable how he's backed us into a corner. I told our guys to settle–I'm tired of the whole thing."

"But everything's going to work out all right? Thanks to ENNU?"

"Right," answered Andrew.

"That's probably the best think that happened to me all year. There's no justice in this business, but that was justice."

After Simon Slater had fired WJR/Chicago he made several other irrational moves, trying to change almost every policy, procedure and vendor. The ENNU owners were appalled and fired him after six months. Sensibly, they promoted the VP of marketing (the one senior executive who hadn't been axed.) One of his first acts was to re-hire WJR/Chicago. Andrew was elated. Three months later, however, ENNU declared its plan to go global. Andrew was worried. Here we go again. This time we'll get caught in a global situation.

He consulted Sandy Bunker–they had become golfing pals–and together they decided to set up a working alliance with Sir George Helmsley and H&H. Bunker counseled that it might lead to something more. It had.

Andrew was now in negotiations with Sir George and a bank of lawyers to merge WJR and H&H. In reality, WJR was being acquired but it would remain autonomous in the states. While Andrew was at first reluctant to proceed, H&H would provide the infusion of cash WJR needed, and the global network that WJR also needed. The good news was that ENNU was pleased.

"What's unbelievable to me is the way you and Eric have gotten along."

"Well, you know I always handled those crusty old chief petty officers in the Navy. Actually, he's turned out to be a big help to me. He's really taken a lot of the admin junk off my back."

"Well, that's what he did all those years for Will, right?"

"I hope he's moving along on the rules and stuff for the "Norman Steinberg employee of the year award."

"That was really a nice idea, honey."

"Yeah. I thought so. And the $20,000 cash is going to get everyone's attention."

"What are you going to call it?"

"Well, because it's an award for achievement in helping grow the company – move WJR forward—I've come up with a name that seems appropriate, "The Norman Conquest.""

"He probably would have liked that," said Sally, with a smile.